PRETTY THUGS 3

SA'ID SALAAM

"Y'all sure y'all don't want me to sing back up?" Lacrecia offered again as they headed out of the dorm. She was just about to belt out her rendition of a Whitney Houston song until she saw the drunken girl staggering towards them. It was nothing spectacular since lots of drunken girls staggered around on the weekends. Except this one was holding a gun in her hand.

"Please no," Penny pleaded and laughed. She was the first one to notice when Lacrecia's face went white from shock. Lacrecia opened her mouth to warn them but no words would come out.

"The heck wrong with you lil girl?" Zenobia asked and drew Callie's attention to her as well. No one else saw Gerty in the flow of girls coming and going and raising the gun.

Gerty had decided Penny was the cause of all of her problems and focused her blurred rage on her. Except she saw three of her since the drugs and alcohol had her seeing triple. She was only feet away as she raised the gun at the middle one and took aim at her chest. Her eyes closed and she squeezed the trigger.

"They shooting!" someone screamed like it was screamed a couple times a week since 'they' were always shooting, or fighting. Usually because 'they' said or 'they' heard. Whoever 'they' are, keeps a lot of shit stirred up. By now the battle weary girls knew to hit the deck.

"What the..." Penny fussed as she hit the hard concrete below.

"Stay down!" Callie screamed in between the shots that were still ringing out. Chips of concrete flew as bullets peppered the ground near their heads since that's what Gerty was shooting at.

"Ow!" Zenobia shrieked in pain and touched her arm. Warm blood filled her hand. "I'm hit!"

"Fuck ass white bitch!" Gerty shouted as she stood over Penny. This time she didn't close her eyes before pulling the trigger inches from her face. Penny starred up into the barrel and accepted her fate. Her short life flashed before her eyes as she waited for the flash that would send her rushing off into the afterlife.

'Click, click, click' the gun said harmlessly.

"Uh-oh!" Gerty said when she realized she had run out of bullets. Heads began to lift and look with each click.

"Uh-oh is right!" Callie growled as she rose to her feet. She was joined by others who had scrambled for cover when the shooting stopped. Gerty tried to make a run for it but didn't make it. She managed to reach the car but the mob was on her ass.

"Un-uh!" a girl declared as she snatched her away from the car. Gerty tried to make a run for it but got tripped and landed on her face. The concrete was far more gentle than the flurry of kicks and stomps that followed.

"I'm hit!" Zenobia repeated as she sat up. Blood flowed between her fingers as she held the wound.

"Let me see!" Callie demanded. "Girl you cut yourself on the ground!"

"Awe man!" she moaned like not getting shot was bad news. "Shoot I was finna be like them niggas showing off where they got shot!"

Penny wanted to see too but had to get Lacrecia off of her so she could get up herself. Everyone else had already gotten back up besides these two. Most were on Gerty's ass, some called it a night and went back in, while others continued on to their destinations. Except these two hadn't budged.

"Uh, lil girl!" Penny fussed, using the new name Zenobia had dubbed up. She may be a doctor one day but today she was lil girl. Except she wasn't responding to anything at the moment. The warm blood soaking them both explained why. "Oh shit! She's shot!"

"Lil girl!" Zenobia shouted as they rolled her off of Penny. A pool of blood began to spread from a hole in the middle of her shirt.

"Call 9-11!" Penny suggested but only because she wasn't from the hood.

"Fuck that!" Callie corrected and ran towards the parking lot. Zenobia pressed on the wound until Callie barreled right up onto the sidewalk.

"Pop the hatch!" Penny shouted and banged on the back window. Callie complied and hit the button to raise the back door. The rush of adrenaline helped the girls load her into the cargo compartment. Penny and Zenobia climbed in with her to protect her from rolling around like groceries.

Atlanta is an extremely violent city which in turn gave them one of the best trauma centers in the country. Grady hospital specialized in gunshot wounds just like the one in Lacrecia's chest. They pulled right up to the emergency room exit and ignored the protest of cops and ambulance drivers.

"You can't park here!" an officer demanded but took a moment to check her out.

"Man, fuck you! My friend is shot!" she shouted back while her friends pulled the limp teen from the truck. The cop backed off when he saw the bloody teen being pulled from the rear. A nurse came out and helped the girls get her inside.

"No, no! Straight to surgery!" a doctor shouted when he saw the wounded child. She took precedence over the leg and arm shots waiting. Most of them were busy on their phones anyway so they didn't mind.

"You guys can't come," a nurse told the girls as they tagged along. Callie started to snap again but Penny reeled her in.

"Sis, let them do their thing," she urged and pulled her back.

"Not unless you finna operate!" Zenobia snapped. She was mad at themselves for what happened to the teen. "This is our fault!"

"Naw, we didn't shoot no gun! This is Gerty damn fault! If she didn't steal our shit, we wouldn't have whooped her ass!" Penny shouted, The anger had to share space with sorrow as a tear leaked from her eye. "I'm tired of people taking shit from me!"

"Me too," Callie admitted softly. Zenobia had taken just as many losses as the rest and said so with a sigh. Their mutual loss was too heavy to stand so they sat with the other family and patients waiting in the waiting room.

"Here you go," the cop said and handed Callie her keys. She looked thoroughly confused so he explained. "I parked it for you."

"Thanks," she said and turned back to her sorrow. They weren't done with police for the night since all gun shots require a police report. There were so many shootings in this city the hospital had detectives assigned there. They were making their way around the room interviewing potential witnesses.

"Dang," Zenobia exclaimed when she realized she was still clutching Lacrecia's phone. She and Callie had both left their own phones in the truck.

"We need to call her parents," Penny suggested and nodded her friend's head. "Gotta unlock it."

"I'm willing to bet that child ain't got a lock on her phone," Callie dared. Zenobia proved her right when the phone opened right up. 'Mom and Dad' was the first number assigned right before theirs and no others.

"Here," Zenobia said and extended the phone to Callie but Callie tucked her hands behind her back to decline.

"Un-uh!" Penny said forcefully and shook her head. Zenobia twisted her lips and made the call.

"Lacrecia?" her mother asked since the girl was usually in bed by this time. As far as she knew but either way, she never called past supper.

"No, um this is um, Zenobia. I go to school with your daughter..." was as far as Zenobia got before she heard the phone drop.

"Hello?" Lacrecia's dad asked as he slipped his slippers off to put on his shoes.

"Yeah, um I go to school with um..." she stammered but her dad wasn't the stammering type and cut right through to the chase.

"Is my daughter dead?" he asked. Starting at the worst case scenario would make anything less that much better. Even Zenobia was relieved to report she wasn't.

"No sir! She's in surgery now. Grady hospital..." she relayed.

"We're on our way," he reported as his wife handed him the keys.

"What they say?" Callie asked when Zenobia pulled the phone from her face.

"They are on their way," she reported. Curiosity got the best of her since the phone was open. "Bet her lil ass got some dick pics?"

"A 'huned says she don't!" Callie challenged.

"I got a hundred on that!" Penny added as Zenobia went to the gallery.

"Two hundred dang dollars worth of dang kittens!" she said, shaking her head. Lacrecia had hundreds of cute cat memes and not nare a dick.

"That's cool, I got enough dick pics to make up for her," Penny consoled and pulled up her own gallery. They were perusing through her payload of penises when someone walked up.

"That looks like me?" a man announced and turned his

head sideways as he looked at the dick pic. Callie opened her mouth to snap and saw the badge on his hip. Then snapped anyway.

"The fuck is wrong with you?" she not only asked but winced up at him to see if she could see what the fuck is wrong with him.

"And youold enough to be our father!" Zenobia added.

"And our friend just got shot! So, what the fuck you want?" Penny tossed in as well.

"Who shot her is what we want to know?" he asked and already began writing. "No one saw the shooter. Just heard shots..."

Ironically Gerty was being wheeled in on a gurney with a freshly whipped ass. The busted head and broken bones needed to be tended to before she could go to jail. She squinted over at her targets while they glared back. Someone would eventually testify against the girl but it wouldn't be them.

"Is that all?" the cop asked after closing his pad. He took their glares as an answer and moved on to the next shooting witnesses. They didn't see anything either though. The girls busied themselves with small talk while awaiting some news. As well as Lecrecia's family to arrive.

"That's them," Zenobia said and nodded towards the worried family walking into the hospital. They saw quite a few worried families walk in but this one had a woman who looked like she could be Lacrecia's older sister. She was an only child so it had to be her mother.

"What y'all looking at me for?" Callie fussed and shook her head. Her friends always looked to her to take the lead, so she did. "Excuse me, Lecrecia's mom and dad?"

"And granddaddy," the older man answered on behalf of all. The preacher's collar around his neck said he did most of the speaking for the family. Generally that is because her mom took the lead now.

"What happened? Where is she? How is she?" the woman demanded. Callie wasn't sure where to begin but the doctor came out and stole the show.

"Who's here for Miss McCoy?" he announced, looking around the waiting room.

"Here!" Mrs McCoy proclaimed and rushed towards him with husband and father in law by her side. "How is she?"

"Fine. Lost a lot of blood, but she'll be fine," he relayed and explained how the bullet missed vital organs.

"We need to see her!" someone demanded. All heads turned around to see who made the demand. Except Penny since it was her. The events had played back in her head a few times so she was sure. "She saved my life!"

"She's awake but needs rest," the doctor said. "I'm limiting visits to immediate family only, and only for a few minutes."

"Go on up. I'll talk to her in the 'mawnin," Pastor McCoy offered and stayed back. Back with the young gals. He watched his son and daughter in law until the elevator door closed. Then looked the girls over like searching for scripture. "Lawd have mercy!"

"Hello Mr McCoy," the girls sang in unison like a chorus. The pastor licked his lips as he looked them over like a fat man does a McDonald's menu.

"I'm going to grab a soda!" Callie blurted and took off.

"I'll help carry them!" Zenobia shouted and took off after her, leaving Penny with the pastor.

"Well youse a pretty lil thang," he vowed like it was an oath. An oath sealed by another lick of his thick lips like an envelope.

"Thank you," Penny said humbly since he was a man of the cloth and all. She was about to find out what he used that cloth for though.

"Let me suck that pussy," he whispered. Then he was going to use that same cloth to wipe the pussy juice off his thick lips.

"Pastor got hoes," she laughed and walked off. Not that he cared since there were more grieving families around. He made his rounds to shoot his shot like a true shooter shoots shots.

"Nuh-uh?" Callie dared when Penny joined them blushing. "I know he ain't try you?"

"Yeah he did! Offered to eat me out," she said and shook her head.

"See, I be wrong if I made him empty them collection plates!" Zenobia chuckled. They got another good laugh when pastor McCoy caught him one and went out to the car.

"Look like she beat you to it. Let's go home," Callie sighed. Their friend was out of the woods and they couldn't see her tonight so nothing more could be done tonight.

"Yeah," Zenobia agreed and followed her friends from the waiting room.

"Amen," Penny cracked when they encountered the pastor returning with the woman. Her legs were wobbly and he was wiping his mouth with his handkerchief. The ensuing laughter died down when they piled into the bloody truck and picked up their bloody phones.

"Shit!" Callie and Zenobia fussed at the missed calls and

missed meetings. Ethan had called Penny but she didn't see it. Dominique had called Callie and Young Vaughn had called Zenobia.

All three turned their phones off. After a night like tonight they weren't in the mood to speak with anyone.

Chapter 2

"Yoooo!" Callie fussed when her phone buzzed for a minute straight as soon as she turned it on Not only was every text, voicemail and DM from Dominique, but she was calling again. "Hello!"

"Thank God! Girl are you OK?" the woman gushed with genuine concern, for her money.

"Yeah?" Callie asked and waited for the other shoe to drop.

"Girl we heard about the shooting last night at the dorm and couldn't get a hold of you?" she continued.

"Yeah we good. Our girl got hit. We getting ready to go back to the hospital now," she relayed while Penny had a similar conversation via text from across the room.

"No problem. Just hit me up and we can meet sometime today," Dominique manipulated smoothly.

"This bitch got all the sense!" Callie fussed when the call ended. Giving someone a choice within parameters is no choice at all.

"What she 'talmbout?" Zenobia asked in between texts with Young Vaughn.

"Still trying to meet up," she relayed and looked over to Penny.

"Same place, same time," she confirmed. Callie sent the details over to Dominique and got up to get ready. The girls performed their synchronized dance of hygiene and wardrobe in the small space. They had it down to a science and set off to check on Lacrecia.

"Pretty Thugs!" a freshman cheered when the crew stepped outside. She fawned and gushed like they were already celebrities. In this viral age of instant fame they were well on their way.

"Put some respeck on our name!" P-money declared, causing her friends to shake their heads.

Callie pulled out her keys so the others followed to her truck. She was a girl so she wasn't expected to open doors. The key fob stopped working so she used the key to unlock the driver's door and pop the locks but she didn't make it.

"What?" Zenobia shrieked and rushed to catch Callie when she practically fell away from the vehicle.

"Mmph!" Penny winced when she caught the strong smell of dried blood.

"Voodoo," was all she could get out. The sight of all that blood reminded her of the bloody crime that happened in this same truck.

"We'll take my car," Zenobia offered and steered her over to her parking spot. They placed her in the back seat while Penny rode shotgun. Their own thoughts filled the car with silence as they rode over to the hospital.

"There go Pastor-got-hoes," Callie said and cheered herself up.

"Look like he got another one," Zenobia laughed as the man escorted yet another woman to the car.

"I guess that means shorty is good," Penny added as they piled out of the car. The waiting room was filled with new faces since the emergency room was filled with new victims.

Slavery may be over but the black race still carried the scars. Broken men looked up to their slave masters so much they wanted to be just like them. Master used to come down to slave row and fuck any of the women he wanted. In turn, black men do the same under the notion of having hoes and being players.

Those masters made babies they neither supported or acknowledged. These niggas do the same. These same niggasloved their masters so much they shared their hatred of themselves. The hate ran so deep, niggaskilled other niggas for wearing a different color on the same black skin. The results of that filled trauma centers, morgues and prisons from coast to coast.

"There go the doctor..." Zenobia smiled when the same doctor came out looking for family. The somber look on his face aged him beyond the few hours they had last seen him.

"Damn," Callie sighed when he delivered news to a young parent that made her wail. "Man let's get the fuck out of here!"

"Chill ma," Penny said and steered her back towards the elevator. "Lil mama took a bullet for me. For us!"

"Yeah, but how do you go from ma, to lil mama?" Zenobia laughed at her mismatched accents.

"Cuz, y'all confusing me!" she laughed and entered the elevator. A few moments later they exited the floor and headed to the nurses station. Callie stepped up and asked for Lecrecia's room.

"Her parents are in with her," the woman advised after pointing out the room number.

"As long as granddad ain't in there," Penny grimaced.

"With his nasty ass!" the nurse concurred and cracked everyone up. The girls were still wearing that same smile when they entered the room.

"No," the father stated, then expounded. "Un-uh, you girls do not need to be in here!"

"Those are my friends daddy!" Lacrecia fussed, making one of the machines beep. "They are the ones who brought me to the hospital! I would still be on the ground if not for them!"

"I..." he began but her mother cut in before he could finish.

"Thank you for bringing her here," the woman offered sincerely since she knew her daughter would have bled to death if she hadn't gotten here when she did. "Let her see her friends and go find your daddy."

"Better find him a toothbrush..." Penny said as they left the room. The room was silent until they were out of sight, then erupted.

"Hey girl! You good? What drugs they got you on?" they all spoke at once.

"I'm good," Lacrecia smiled. She was giddy to have the whole crew in her hospital room. They may be minor celebrities but they were her friends. Her only friends.

"So when you getting up out this piece?" Zenobia asked, looking at the machines like she was ready to unhook them.

"Another day, for observation," she reported happily, but a 'but' quickly changed her face.

"What?" Zenobia asked urgently.

"I was pregnant," she said just above a whisper. The look of shame on her face came back and pushed a tear from her eye.

"Was?" Callie asked hopefully since sometimes 'was' is better than 'am'. Like, I 'was' broke is better than I 'am' broke. This was one of those sometimes.

"The blood loss..." Lacrecia explained like it was explained to her.

"Ice?" Penny needed to know. The guttural growl in her tone turned heads towards her.

"Who else!" Callie snapped and turned to the girl to confirm. "Right?"

"Right, but..." Lacrecia sighed.

"But what lil girl!" Zenobia fussed.

"No but like that! I really pushed it out of my head. The rape," she said and turned to Penny who told her to do so. It may not have been the best advice to get through a trauma but it was all she had. Would have worked too if not for that one damn sperm finding that egg.

"But what then?" Callie asked.

"I gotta go home," she pouted. "My dad says I can't go to Atlanta college no more."

"So how you gonna be a doctor!" Zenobia shot back and looked out the door for this daddy of hers. Lecrecia's shoulders shrugged since that part hadn't been dictated to her yet.

"Uh oh..." Penny chuckled when she saw the McCoy's on their way back to the room. She sank into the chair to get a good seat for the impending fireworks display.

"OK girls...." Mrs McCoy began as they entered. It was determined she would be the spokesman since she was a female.

"How the fu..." Zenobia barked, but Callie cupped her mouth and took over.

"Look, I respect the fact that you want to keep your child safe," she opened.

"You can't. Or you wouldn't be about to say anything about how we, her parents, chose to do that," Mrs McCoy said firmly. Penny nodded and almost clapped at the smooth clap back but she was on the wrong team.

"I respect that," Callie nodded and fell back. She didn't have and wasn't planning on having any kids, anytime soon, but was pretty sure she wouldn't want some strangers telling her how to raise them.

"I don't! Fuck that!" Zenobia snapped. "This girl is on her way to becoming a doctor and you are stopping her!"

"Stopping her from dying!" her father spoke up. His wife fell back now and let her leader lead the way. "Now, your parents might think getting pregnant and shot is a part of the college experience, but we don't."

The man hit a mental mute button since the room went eerily quiet. Mentioning parents to people who don't have any can have that effect. Penny pouted at the recent loss of the last of her ancestors. Zenobia only had a father but he was buried alive in the prison system. Callie had it worse since she had no idea whose nose she had or where she got the dimples from.

"I can see you are some good girls. And you care about my daughter," Mrs McCoy added softly since she saw her husband strike a nerve.

"We do," Callie croaked and tried not to cry.

"Then come up to the house any time. Lacrecia will transfer to a local school and live at home," the woman explained to them, while looking at her daughter. Lacrecia nodded in acquiescence and accepted her fate.

"Any time! Come any time," Pastor McCoy reiterated and licked his lips. There were more tears and hugs as the girls said their 'so longs' and 'see you laters'. They hugged Lacrecia in her bed and then her mother.

"Daddy..." Mrs McCoy said sternly when the pastor held his arms open for a hug too. She had no doubt he would grab a booty or two so she cut him short.

"Mmhm, yes Lawd," he agreed and settled for looking at those booties as they shifted out of the room.

Chapter 3

"*T*hat trick is ready to re-up," Callie laughed when she received the text from Savage.

"You got him?" Zenobia asked hopefully since she didn't like dealing with him after her slip up that allowed his tongue to slip up inside of her.

"Not unless you want to?" she shot back for the same reason. He had become extra needy after she rejected him.

"Shit, I'll go. I need my dick sucked anyway," Penny laughed. They talked about him just like dudes do a known slut.

"All these dudes really be hoes," Zenobia offered seriously. "Jump in they DM and say, 'you cute' and they'll let you fuck."

"The fuck is wrong with you!" Callie squealed and they all cracked up. She turned back to Penny when the laughter died down. "On the strength tho, you can. I gotta go the other way to take care of Brandon."

"Yeah, and I gotta meet that stud. My daddy sending her for a couple pounds," Zenobia added. They had already swung by the storage and picked up enough pounds to make their rounds. Now it was time to make pickups and deliveries.

"This gone dead us. I'll call when we get in," Penny advised since they were about to run out of weed.

"We still gotta meet with them folks later," Zenobia reminded of the meeting with the record execs.

"Fuck them folks," Callie semi mumbled. "This is how we eat!"

She was just as excited about their potential but being raised in foster care sometimes limited her vision to what was directly in front of her. Zenobia opened her mouth to add her two cents but a knock on the door stole their attention. Everyone looked around at everyone else to see who was expecting anyone to come knocking. No one was so they all raced to the door and snatched it open while wearing matching mean mugs on their faces.

"Mmhm. Yeah," Dean Jenkins said as he walked in on top of them. His secretary stood back like a body guard since that's exactly what she was. Except to guard the student's bodies from him since her job was dependant on his. He cradled a bucket of wings under his arm like a little girl holds her baby doll.

"Can we help you Dean, sir?" Callie asked as he stepped fully into the dorm and looked around. He slid a flat into his mouth and let his secretary answer while he stripped all the meat from the bone with his mighty suction.

"According to rule 21-8-9, staff can and will inspect any living quarters between the hours..." she recited verbatim.

"Smell like, reefers?" he asked and sniffed the air.

"Who? What? Huh?" the girls asked since no one under forty five called them reefers anymore.

"Mary Jane," he explained but that too was beyond their time on earth as well. No worries, he worked a drum while his help helped out.

"Pressure, gas," she said in their language.

"We do not smoke weed!" Penny proudly proclaimed on behalf of them all.

"Naw, but I heard y'all sell it," the dean nodded while he continued looking around. He didn't lift or touch anything but was hoping for a glimpse of some panties.

"Who? Us? Nuh-uh!" the girls replied on top of each other. Even though the backpack he was looking at on the spare bed had a couple of pounds in it. As did the one on Callie's back and the one in Zenobia's hand. Penny was ready to claim it if he picked it up but he looked over it in his search for panties.

"Mmhm," he hummed and worked another flat. He slid it in fat and full, and slid it out stripped and clean a second later. His secretary blushed as proof of what that mouth do. "But that's not why I'm here."

Each one of these smart girls knew full well he expected them to ask why he was here. They were equally smart asses too so no one did. That got a smirk out of the lady in the hallway.

"Thought I told y'all gals no more fighting?" he asked but it really wasn't a question since he answered for them. "I did. I shole did."

"You did," his secretary cosigned when he looked to her for a cosigner. She was a cosigner, hype man and door dash all in one.

"And we ain't been fighting!" Zenobia pleaded their case to her but she nodded at him.

"Seems there is a virus going 'round, with y'all name on

it!" he declared plainly but once again no one knew what he was talking about. All heads turned to the woman in the hall for explanation.

"He means viral. The video," she said and pulled it up on her tablet. There was P-money setting off a near riot in a club.

"Oooooh!" the girls all sang.

"But, that's not on campus!" Callie stressed. Surely he had no say on what happened anywhere off campus.

"No, y'all just get into shootouts on campus," he shot back between a flat and a drum. The stripped down carcass of a flat slipped from his saucy fingers. All eyes followed it to the ground expecting him to pick it up. He didn't, and went on. "An alumni just pulled his daughter out of school. She got shot!"

"We didn't shoot her!" Penny insisted. "She was our friend!"

"And still she got shot," he reiterated.

"So, what are you saying?" Callie snapped. Her phone was buzzing in her purse and there was money to make.

"I'm saying, one more incident..." Dean Jenkins was saying but the woman cut it with the correction.

"Sir, this was the one more incident..." his secretary reminded.

"Oh yeah!" he laughed and popped his own head like people do when they could have had a V8 but didn't.

"Oh yeah what?" Callie fussed when her phone buzzed again.

"You gotta go. End of the semester you three have to leave," he remembered. All mouths dropped since no one saw that coming.

"We're getting kicked out of school?" Zenobia moaned as if it was the end of the world.

"No, just the dorm," the woman in the hall answered.

"Unless," the Dean announced and paused, "Unless I find out you guys really are selling cheeba-cheeba!"

"Weed," the secretary added before they turned to her. "Just stay out of trouble girls. Your grades are great! Just..."

"Y'all just wild! Calm down, chill out," Dean Jenkins said as he turned to leave.

"Wait!" Callie shouted before he could get too far. Now all eyes turned to her to see what was so urgent. She calmly reached down to pick up the bone. Then politely dropped it in the empty bucket.

"Sho nuff," the Dean laughed and waddled away.

"What we supposed to do now?" Zenobia wanted to know.

"What we've been doing. Getting money!" Callie shot back quickly.

"Word!" Penny added and picked up her bag. They all headed out but only two headed to the parking lot. Callie took off on foot over to Brandon's dorm while the others drove off to their destinations.

"Who!" Savage called into the intercom since Penny had her back turned. Her reply was simply to turn around. He responded by hitting the button to buzz her in.

"Don't play with me..." Penny laughed to herself as she headed over to the elevator bank. When it arrived she checked herself out in the ankle length sundress and sandals. Women need to complement each other but especially themselves. "Cutie!"

"Hey, come on in," Savage said as she arrived. She had heard about the gray shorts with the lump and now got to see for herself.

"A'ight..." she laughed as she came in. Little did he know she was notorious when it came to playing games. This could be a simple drug deal or not, his choice.

"Let me get this bread," he said and disappeared into the back. Penny took the opportunity to pull out the weed and her phone. She opened the app and sat it down before he returned . He obviously gave the dick a few pulls since it was more pronounced when he returned. "Here you go."

"And there you go..." she said in return and counted up the money.

"I wonder what it tastes like..." he offered while she counted. She let the first one go but he came back with more. "Some white girl pussy. Never tasted that before."

"Taste like chicken," Penny mused and laughed at her own joke.

"I love chicken! Can I get a taste?" he asked and hit her with that killer smile. That smile had gotten him into a lot of vaginas but it was going to get him into trouble one day.

"Mmm, maybe..." she said as she wrapped up the count. It was good money so business was concluded. Now for a little pleasure. "Let me see your di..."

"Here!" he presented the dick before she completed the question. Good thing she wasn't about to ask for a dictionary because all he had was a handful of dick.

"Get it hard. Let me see wha..." she began but again he beat her to it and started stroking his dick.

"You like that?" he dared seductively as he pulled his pecker.

"Mmhm, twist your wrist," she directed since she was actually directing. Her growing number of followers were getting a live show on her account.

"Like, sssss that?" he asked as he complied. She hiked her dress up to give him a nice crotch shot which helped him stroke a little faster. He got so caught up in showing off he was inching closer to the edge. Penny knew the signs when his knees buckled. It wouldn't be seen on camera so she pulled her panties to the side and... "Shit!"

"Shit!" Penny agreed when an arch of ejaculate headed straight for her. She managed to scramble out of the way but the money didn't make it.

"Fuck!" he grunted and milked himself dry. "You got the prettiest pussy I ever saw."

"Mmhm," she agreed and scooped the money into the bag. He was saying something else about something but she was on her way out the door. "Of course I do. Pretty thug shit!"

"HEY MA, WHAT'S GOOD?" ROZZ GREETED WHEN SHE opened the door for Callie. She may have been from Missouri but after a few months of dating Brandon she was sounding more like a New Yorker with each day.

"You chica," Callie shot back to show her how that Harlem shit should sound.

"Yooo!" Brandon cheered as he looked up from counting money. He already had the count but just liked counting it. He had a stack of hundreds and fifties to pay what he owed. Another stack of twenties, tens and fives was for him. While the ones went to wifey. Her new Gucci purse was stuffed with bills.

"Yo yourself papi," Callie shot back while Rozz committed a new word to her up top repertoire. She began to empty the pounds from her back pack and replaced them with the racks. Her mind had been made up on the walk over so she retrieved her keys and removed the vehicle keys. "I need a couple things from you..."

"What's up?" he asked and looked over to the rows of Jordan's under his bed. He was ready to slip a pair of them on and carry out whatever she needed done.

"I need the whip cleaned out," she said but left the part about cleaning blood. Mainly because it wouldn't matter.

"Gotcha ma. What else?" he asked since he knew she didn't regulate him to washing her car. He was going to pay his roommate a few bucks to handle that anyway. "You said a couple things. That's one?"

"Oh yeah. Once it's clean, keep it, It's yours," she said and turned to leave. Not before getting mobbed by Brandon and Rozz. They wrapped her in hugs, kisses and thanks. "A'ight, A'ight. Cuz I know where y'all mouths have been!"

"Thanks ma. For real, for real..." Brandon choked up. People who have never been given shit in life usually appreciate shit more than people who have. Some people didn't have shit because they don't appreciate shit. Fuck them people.

"Yeah, yeah," Callie said and turned before she got choked up. The door opened and Brandon threw the comforter over the weed as roommate Rufus walked in.

Callie nodded since the kid knew something was going on, just not the extent.

"H,h,hey C,c,Callie," the teen stammered. Callie gave him something to stutter about when she planted a soft kiss on his lips. He was stuck in place for a minute after the door closed behind him.

"Rufus! You good bro?" Brandon laughed and unstuck the kid.

"Huh?" the kid asked when he came to. He didn't have time to wait for an answer though. He grabbed his lotion and rushed straight into the bathroom.

"Eww!" Rozz squealed while Brandon cracked up.

"Gotta get that boy some pussy!" he laughed and shook his head.

"You finna get you some too papi!" added quickly and smiled at using her new word.

Chapter 4

"What the fuck is this?" Callie asked when she encountered the slimy money.

"Yeah, might wanna wash your hands!" Zenobia cracked since she watched the live show while waiting on the corrections officer.

"What?" Callie asked as Penny pulled up the answer.

"I took it down," Penny advised but was in for a shock.

"Don't matter. That thang went viral!" Zenobia shot back. Her eyes went wide when she saw thousands of shares and tens of thousands of comments.

"That thang!" Callie laughed when Savage appeared on screen, dick in hand. Her vagina gave a reminiscing throb when she saw it. She tilted her head and watched with enthusiasm and recognized the face he made just before he skeeted the answer to her question of what was on the money. "Ewww!"

"That chic is really crazy!" Zenobia laughed and shook her head at her friend. They got back to the task of counting money.

"Wow," Penny proclaimed. She came from money but it was her father's. Hustling it up on your own really hits different.

"I know right," Callie concurred. "Call ole boy when we get back so we can flip it again."

"I need some thangs..." Zenobia declared and peeled off a couple grand. She twisted her lips at the paltry pile, then peeled off two thousand more.

"Sounds about right," Penny agreed and counted out five grand for herself. As soon as she finished Callie moved in and did the same.

"May as well keep it even," Callie decided and counted out five thousand for herself and another grand for her friend. There was still plenty to re-up and stash some cash in the storage unit.

"We finna be late," Zenobia addressed the elephant in the room. The meeting was in a few minutes but they hadn't budged yet. It usually took them more time than they had to get ready.

"Yeah," Callie decided and put an end to the procrastination by hopping to her feet.

"Are we going like this?" Penny asked as she hopped up as well.

"May as well," she shrugged and led the way out of the room.

"Where yo whip at B?" Zenobia shrieked when she saw the empty spot where Callie's truck should be.

"Brandon got it," she said without explaining the rash decision that lead to him having it.

Penny hit the key fob and popped her locks. They piled into the Benz and pulled away from the dorm. Zenobia reached up between the seats and turned the radio on. Just in time to hear the occupants of the car singing the hook on the hottest new song in the city. That meant turning it all the way up as they rode to the restaurant.

"We're late," Zenobia said when she spotted Mike's Porsche parked in the front of the lot. There was no valet so he pulled in cockeyed and took up two spaces so no one could get close enough to ding his doors. A luxury Penny didn't have at the dorms and had the dents and dings to prove it.

"Yeah," Callie said since their plan was to arrive earlier than everyone else. They were still a few minutes ahead of the agreed upon time but Mike still beat them.

"Well, let's see what shawty 'talmbout," Callie sighed and opened the door.

"Yeah, no, I'ma need you not to say that no more!" Zenobia fussed and cracked them all up. The good laugh broke the tension they all felt.

"There they go," Mike mentioned and nodded towards the still smiling crew. He looked down at the bag of cash on the seat and nodded confidently.

"Yeah," Dominique said and fought the urge to correct him, since they were coming, not going. A snake can shed its whole skin so changing her snarl to a smile was no problem. "Hey girls!"

"Hey Dominique!" they sang. They kept the same pitch when they turned to Mike and sang to him as well. "Hey Mike!"

"Sup," he greeted gruffly like this was a drug deal. A swift kick under the table reminded him that it wasn't. "You ladies look nice,"

"Nuh-uh! No we don't! We ain't even change!" they gushed in the compliment.

Dominique caught Callie glancing around and would bet it all she was looking for Lil Bruh. Mike actually suggested bringing him along to help sway her but she quickly reminded him they were offering the girls the same thing they gave him.

A hundred thousand dollars was a decent advance for some chicks who only sang a hook. Lil Bruh was rapping in traps and jails his whole young life. He had a nice buzz in the streets before Mike pulled him into the studio. He took that hundred grand and bought a car, a chain and more coke to sell back in Jersey.

"Well, you know why we're here," Dominique cut in. "It's no secret that you girls are talented. With our help, we can make you stars!"

Zenobia's eyes lit up at the prospect of being a star. Stars have clout and she would use that clout to free her father. Luckily there was no contract on the table because she was ready to sign. Not Callie though since she had been studying. The red in her eyes was from spending most of the night between Google and YouTube, taking a crash course in the music industry.

"How?" Callie asked to keep her talking. Even liars will run out of lies if they talk long enough. Then have no choice but to speak the truth.

"We have the hottest producers in the game! Best writers to write all your songs!" she cheered while Mike nodded. The girls remained stoic so she had to go on. "And, check out the image we decided on..."

"I'm not wearing that!" Callie shrieked when Dominique turned the iPod in her direction. The model mainly modeled whatever lotion she wore since she barely had any clothing on. She squat wide legged like the iconic

Lil Kim poster. Dominique assumed she spoke for the rest but came to find out she only spoke for herself.

"That's hot!" Penny gushed when she came to look over her shoulder.

"Ooh that is nice! I'd rock the hell out of that!" Zenobia cosigned. Callie was clearly outvoted but this wasn't a democracy.

"Rock it cuz I ain't!" Callie demanded.

"We'll worry about the clothes later!" Mike huffed and cut to the chase. He reached for the bag since it was filled with cash. The plan was to dump it out on the table but another kick under the table slowed him up. "Fuck you keep kicking me for?"

"Cuz..." Dominique said and nodded towards the door. Mike turned and saw Ethan step inside and look around. He looked utterly confused when his eyes met Mike's, then saw Penny and the other girls. Confusion turned to amusement when he caught on.

"Knew she was a smart girl," he mumbled to himself as he made his way over. Penny was shrewd but this had Callie written all over it.

"Hey!" Penny cheered and relinquished her seat when he reached the table. She grabbed another from the next table of four since only three people were seated.

"The fuck you doing here?" Mike barked around the table.

"Same as you I suspect," Ethan answered and turned to the ringleader before finishing. "I assume the ladies would like to explore all options?"

"We would," Callie concurred and turned back to Mike and the bag. "You were saying?"

"Let's hear what the white boy got to say!" Mike

demanded. Dominique looked at the white girl they were trying to sign and shook her head.

"Well, obviously I see the value in what the ladies have to bring," Ethan said and laid a sample contract on the table in front of the crew. "Industry standard."

"Let me see this shit!" Mike said and snatched the paperwork before Callie could see it. She still had questions of her own while Mike read through the contract he couldn't beat. He could certainly match it if he wanted to. He didn't though because he planned to take advantage of these girls just like the rest of the artists on his label.

"So, you guys want to write all of our songs too?" Callie dared.

"You'd be crazy to let someone else write your songs! You would miss out on millions of dollars in publishing!" he shot back. "Plus, you girls are the draw! Whatever you bring will hit!"

"We gotta dress like prostitutes?" Callie asked and lifted her chin royally. She liked to look cute, sexy even, but wasn't 'bussin it open for the world to see.

"I told y'all we'll get back to the image!" Mike interjected. He still wanted them to dress like prostitutes though. He would control every aspect of their lives if they signed with him.

"I like you guys as you are," Ethan added. The girls were fly every time he saw them. Plus they were viral already, why switch up.

"What about if we went independent?" Callie added. Both Penny and Zenobia to snap their heads in her direction. Even Callie wasn't exactly sure what all it meant but Brandon had been babbling about some rapper who just turned down a major label deal and stayed independent. The look on Mike's face said it was something.

"You have that option," Ethan nodded. He still looked a little disappointed but would keep it a hundred. "You'll still need distribution."

"And management!" Dominique spoke up. Mike looked like he wanted to flip the table over but she patted his leg under the table. Their management contracts were just as treacherous as their record deal. A financial rape on the dotted line.

"You'll need management," Ethan agreed, but only because he offered that service as well.

"We need to discuss how to proceed," Callie decided. She realized the ball was in her court and she would play it like Venus and Serena's daddy.

"Look, review the contract. Explore all your options. Take your time and make the best choice for you. Generational wealth is at stake here." Ethan said and stood. He nodded to all and turned to leave.

"Yeah, get the fuck 'outa here white boy!" Mike barked to his back. Dominique kicked him again since he was offending the white girl they were trying to sign. "Kick me again and I'll kick your ass back to Jersey!"

"Mike I..." she pleaded but he stood and marched off with the contract in hand. He was all the way out of the restaurant before Dominique broke the awkward silence. "I'm sorry about all that."

"Don't be," Penny shot back, since what was there to be sorry about. Some black people were just as racist as some white people. That's a fact, so why be sorry about it.

"Like dude said, there is generational wealth at stake here," Callie said apologetically.

"He's right. I just want to help you girls. That's why I sold y'all weed when he refused. I put my ass on the line!" Dominique fussed. It was the only leverage she had so she doubled down on it. "Then, when we pulled out, I put you on with the connect!"

"So, I guess that's dead now huh?" Zenobia challenged.

"Dead as the bird in that tortilla!" she barked, nodding at the half eaten chicken quesadilla appetizers. Penny pulled her phone to text Ramone on the spot.

"So, if we don't fuck with y'all, y'all gonna fuck up our bread?" Callie shot back. Dominique quickly realized she was losing ground and switched gears.

"That's on Mike. Remember, I had to convince him to do business in the first place," she reminded even though it was she who made the call that pulled the plug on their plug.

"Well, like Ethan said, we finna take our time and make the best decision. For us, Ion care who don't like it," Zenobia insisted.

"Sounds good," Dominique agreed since she had no choice. "Just remember who has been on your side from day one!"

"Yeah," Callie agreed. She was correct and had been on their side. They had tens of thousands of dollars to show for it. "Do you need a ride?"

"Nah, I'll get an Uber," Dominique sighed and shook her head. Mike was turning into someone she didn't recognize once major money came into play.

"We'll holla," Penny said and chunked deuces as she stood. As far as she was concerned this would be the last time having to see the woman.

"Peace," Callie added while Zenobia had nothing to say.

"Callie..." Dominique called before they got too far. Perfectly timed to ensure the others couldn't hear her parting words to Callie.

"Sup ma?" she asked, but only turned partially towards her since turning all the way required turning her back to her friends. Something she would never do.

"Look," she began softly enough not to carry it to her friends. "Never forget who you are, and where you came from. Girl you me at that age. And know you're the star of the show. They are the damn Pips. Fuck with us and we'll give you a solo deal too."

"I hear you," Callie said loud enough for her friends. They couldn't hear the offer but damn sure heard the answer.

"What she 'talmbout?" Zenobia asked with her face scrunched up.

"Nothing. She ain't talkin bout a bitch ass thing," Callie replied while the thoughts of solo stardom still twirled in her mind.

Chapter 5

"Who!" Savage barked into the intercom. Business was good but he was in his feelings about the viral video of him jacking off.

"Davinci. Olly sent me," the new face replied into the speaker. The door buzzed and allowed him entry. A few minutes later he was ringing the doorbell.

"Come on in," Savage sighed as he stepped aside to let the new customer into his house. He was too young to listen to Biggie and didn't know about rule number five. He was here to buy an ounce so he should have told him to bounce.

"Yeah, Olly put me on. I have been buying from him but he says he can't do a whole ounce," he explained.

"Yeah," Savage agreed since he only sold Olly ounces that he broke down to make his profit. "I got whatever you need."

"Is that so?" Davinci asked with a sparkle in his eye. It was telling but Savage couldn't tell.

"Yup," he said and placed four ounces on the table. "Five hundred, each."

"I'll take two for now," the new customer said and produced a thousand dollars of fresh from the bank cash.

"You got the number," Savage said as his phone buzzed again. Something it did every few seconds since the video.

"Business booming I see!" Davinci nodded.

"That and people talking about some damn video!" he sighed and shook his head. It actually turned out to be a good promotion for his hobby of tricking off with as many chicks as possible.

"Oh, yeah," he agreed since he had seen it too. They exchanged dap and he turned to leave. Savage pulled the door open just as a busty blonde reached for the doorbell.

"Oh hey Debbie. Come on in," Savage greeted happily and happily exchanged one visitor for the other. Visitors with vaginas are always the best.

"Business booming indeed!" Davinci nodded as he headed back down the hallway.

"Business booming like fuck!" Zenobia announced when she stepped back into the room. She noticed her partners didn't share her enthusiasm and asked, "What?"

"Ramone ain't hitting back. Won't answer, won't hit back," Callie moaned. She knew why but didn't want to admit it.

"That bitch Dominique pulled the plug on us!" Penny growled since she had no problems with the ugly truth.

"Because we ain't sign with them?" Zenobia asked incredibly.

"Hell yeah, so she's gonna try to put the press on us to make us," Penny spat.

"Don't that bitch know we been under pressure? We fucking diamonds after all the pressure we been through!" Callie moaned. She had been considering the management deal with Dominique but this went too far. "We're gonna find a new plug. Show this bitch we don't need her!"

"I'ma ask Vaughn," Zenobia said which explained the tiny dress laid out on the bed.

"Ooooh, someone getting some action!" Penny teased.

"Maybe some wrist action. How do you do it?" Zenobia asked, making twisting movements with her hand.

"Gotta work the lips too!" she said and placed her hairbrush into her mouth to demonstrate.

"I'm not sucking his dick! I'm quite sure it tastes like pussy," she grimaced.

"And, just how does pussy taste?" Penny asked and cocked her head.

"Girl boo!" she laughed and shook her head. "You just tried me up."

"That's why I ain't called Lil Bruh. What's the point? I'm sure he is getting a lot of pussy. He don't need mine," Callie winced with confusion.

What she didn't get is that it's not about the pussy, per se. It's about different pussy. New pussy, exotic, pussy, hard to get pussy. It's about the chase, the catch and the kill for some dudes. Weak dudes mainly, who are literally slaves to their desires. Those guys will never be content with just one vagina.

"Exactly why my hymen is exactly where it should be!" Penny proudly proclaimed.

"Miss goody two shoes!" Zenobia teased. "Shoot I want some sex too, but I cain't go out bad."

"I'm a goody two shoes too!" Callie laughed. "I've only been with two dudes in my whole life!"

"Two?" both of her friends shot back simultaneously.

"Voodoo and who?" Penny asked and tilted her head. There was a moment of silence while Callie processed her predicament. She spoke so quickly she told on herself.

"Please don't tell me you let Savage hit!" Zenobia demanded with a whole, 'eww' on her face.

"Well, I mean, I let him eat me out. I have to count that right?" she offered to wiggle her way out.

"No!" Penny quickly replied since she didn't have an offhand number of all the guys she let lick her box. She drifted into her head to take a quick count.

"Nah, letting a nigga eat don't go on your body count," Zenobia replied. Hers was higher than she cared to admit since she had a rough spot in life when she lost both parents. Her brother was no help and granny was drunk. Dudes showed her a lot of attention since she was pretty, and yellow and had a fat ass.

"Twelve!" Penny cheered and pumped her fist triumphantly when she reached a number. "Well, thirteen counting Sarah's dad."

"On another note," Zenobia began once the laughter died back down. "What we finna do about this music shit? How much money do you think was in that bag?"

"Don't know, but I do know it's not enough!" Callie reckoned. "He knew it was a chump off too!"

"Word! You see how quick he tucked that shit when Ethan walked in!" Penny laughed.

"OK so, I'm finna see Vaughn tonight. I'm gonna pick his brain. You need to see what Lil Bruh 'talmbout. And you..." Zenobia directed around the room.

"Guess I'll have to let Ethan be number fourteen," Penny pouted like it was a problem as she shot the man a text.

"Awe, poor lil tink, tink!" Zenobia laughed. It was Callie who laughed last as she texted Lil Bruh. A few back and forth texts and they all had dates.

"COME ON!" YOUNG VAUGHN CALLED AT HIS FRONT DOOR in reply to the knock. He was speeding over two hundred miles an hour on the game featured on the massive TV.

"No, don't get up," Zenobia quipped sarcastically as she traipsed inside.

"Huh?" he asked, trying to steal a glance at her while keeping an eye on the virtual road on the screen.

"Nothing..." she declared and left him be. She once had a brother and knew how guys get over their games. In the meanwhile she looked for tracesfemales may have left behind. It would have been hard to see through the dense fog of weed smoke from the blunt smoldering in the ashtray.

"Uh! Oh! I..." Vaughn reeled and reeled as his car swerved. He gained control for a second, then crashed into the wall. "Shit!"

"Mmhm," she hummed when he finally laid both eyes on her.

"Shit!" he proclaimed since she was looking great in the tiny dress that showed off the plump breast and fat ass.

"I know, right!" she giggled when he hopped up and pulled her into an embrace. There were no complaints when his tongue slipped into her mouth. Nor when he scooped her off her feet. In fact, she complied by wrapping her legs around his waist as he carted her off to his bedroom.

"Sexy ass!" he announced when he tossed her sexy ass in the middle of the king sized bed.

"You sexy too!" she declared when he began to strip. She was anticipating to see some dick but he reached his boxer briefs and climbed on the bed. She hadn't made her mind up on how far to go but took control when he tried to climb between her legs. "Un-uh, on your back."

"Shit yeah!" Young Vaughn cheered since he was a man. Men, old and young love for a woman to ride the dick.

"Mmhm," she moaned as they resumed their kiss. She grinded her crotch against his rock hard dick until they both moaned from behind the twirling tongues.

Vaughn reached down and pulled his boxers down to free the dick. Zenobia still hadn't committed when she removed her wet panties. She resumed grinding against the dick until Vaughn reached down to get inside of her.

"Un-uh," she declined and moved his hand away. She gripped his wrist and pinned them to the bed as she grinded. Grinded, grinded until she seized from an intense orgasm.

"Sho nuff?" Vaughn laughed as she squirmed and hissed. She loosed her grip so he gripped her ass and picked up where she left off. Zenobia was limp from busting a nut, but he still slid her slippery box the length of his erection. "Fuck! I'm finna.... Ugh!"

"Sho nuff?" Zenobia laughed when it was his turn to writhe and hiss from busting a pretty good nut of his own. Better than the one he bust from the back shots he delivered to a groupie last night, without even getting inside of Zenobia.

"Hush girl," he laughed and gathered her up in his arms. He may not have said it, but she felt loved at the moment.

"Hey! What's up?" Ethan asked as he opened the door for Penny. He did a double take at the tiny dress with lots of cleavage on display. "Is everything OK?"

"Hey! Yeah, I um, wanted to pick your brain about this whole, group thing?" she sang as she traipsed inside.

"Sure, sure!" he readily agreed and led her to the sofa. "Drink?"

"Yes please," she accepted until he reached for the bottle of brandy on the table. "Oh no, I thought you meant..."

"Coke!" he laughed and popped his head. "Forgot you guys are minors."

"Who sell pounds of weed," she reminded. "We're twenty years old, you know. But, I don't really drink."

"One coke, coming up," Ethan announced and headed into the kitchen. When he returned he schooled her to the music biz. He stole occasional glances at the thick, tanned thighs pressed against the leather sofa as they spoke.

"So, what Callie said. About being independent?" she asked and saw his eyes drop to her legs once again.

"Um...?" Ethan asked when her legs parted just enough to offer a glimpse of the pink panties she wore. He was so distracted he forgot the question. "Huh?"

"Independent? Good idea?" Penny giggled and helped

him out by closing her legs. She had always been a tease but made sure not to write checks her virginity couldn't cash.

"Beautiful! Idea, that is," he said even though he was talking about her legs as well. They both shook it off and got down to business. "You spend your own money to record your project. Itcan be both lucrative as well as risky."

"Risky how?" she asked since a lifetime of affluence had her well versed in lucrative. Life as a Pretty Thug had introduced her to a world of risk.

"It can be rejected. You can spend the money, the label still wants you but not the project," he explained.

"But, if they do like it?" she dared with the confidence he expected from a Pretty Thug.

"Then I will probably offer you a few million to distribute it," he stated plainly. The look on her face was similar to a deer getting caught in headlights so he explained. "An advance that I would recoup from sales. Probably in a few months, then you girls would get eighty percent. I'll keep twenty."

"And a record deal like Mike and Dominique are offering?" she managed to get out even though she was feeling light headed.

"I haven't seen exactly what his contracts state. Probably a couple hundred grand up front. You won't have to pay for production..." he guessed. "I would guess 360, which is modern day slavery."

"I probably better go," Penny decided in a hurry. All this money talk was making her vagina throb. This business was too big to mix with pleasure so she stood.

"Oh, OK. Well, if you guys have any other questions..." he was saying as she rushed from the apartment.

"Wow!" She said down the hall. Down the elevator and all the way back to the dorm. "Just wow!"

Chapter 6

"**W**asn't me,'"Dominique announced when she took Callie's call.

"So y'all gonna cut us off cuz we want what's best for ourselves. Fuck business, I thought we were friends?" Callie whimpered. She had to cover the phone so the woman wouldn't hear her snicker.

"We are friends! I'm trying to look out for you! Been looking out from day one!" she shot back.

"Then why you tryna stop us from eating?" Callie asked and cocked her head like it was a dare.

"Bitch we had a quarter million dollars in the bag! Stop you from eating? We tryna feed yo stubborn ass!" she shot back. Now it was her who had to cover the phone so Mike couldn't be heard.

"Quarter mil? Bitch you lost your mind!" the greedy exec huffed and rolled his eyes. There was a hundred grand in the bag. He would make that a hundred times over if the girls blew up.

"Chill," Dominique told him, then uncovered the

phone. "Look, enjoy your date and we'll talk tomorrow. OK?"

"OK," Callie sighed just as the line went dead. Just in time for the text alerting her that Lil Bruh was out front. She did a final check of her lip gloss and popped her lips at the perfection. She was out in the hallway when she processed Dominique's last statement. "How did this bitch know I had a date tho?"

"You look hot ma!" Lil Bruh said as Callie climbed into the smoke filled cabin of his new Benz. It was one of the first purchases he made with his six figure advance.

"Hot from having to open the door for myself," she quipped but it went over his head. Not just because he was slouched in his seat either.

"Yo, this the song I want y'all on..." he said and turned on the music. Callie's hips betrayed her attitude and started winding on the leather seat. Her head began to nod as she listened to the beat, the rhymes and melody. By the time the chorus came around she ad libbed her own words to it. "Yo! That's crazy!"

"You like that?" she asked unsurely since it was her first time being creative. Young Vaughn had written the hook they did for him but this was her own.

"Love it! You should drop it tonight!" he insisted, making her face hurt from smiling so wide.

"Tonight? I can't. My girls on dates," she sighed.

"Shit, you can do it yourself?" he asked and smiled.

"Ion know..." she moaned and bit the inside of her cheek.

"Just lay it down and they can come in whenever..." he explained as she shot a text out. They had arrived at his condo and no one had hit back yet. Mainly because both Penny and Zenobia were with Ethan and Young Vaughn.

"I guess," she decided by the time they entered the building. It was a freestyle, so it would be better to lay it down before it got away. He led her into the elevator and down the hall to his unit.

"Here we go..." Lil Bruh announced triumphantly as he opened the door.

"This is..." Callie was smiling, ready to compliment until she saw the nearly empty space. "Empty?"

"Need a ladies touch," he said and touched the small of her back as she stepped inside. The touch of a man reverberated through her whole body, causing a quiver in her panties. She had to wonder if Lil Bruh wasn't going to get a lil pussy tonight.

"And amaid," she laughed since the place was single man, messy. Like he tried to clean up but didn't quite understand what clean meant.

"Shit, from the Bricks to this tho!" he said and it was plenty. After a life of poverty in violent Newark, New Jersey. This was a castle in an enchanted forest.

"Word!" Callie concurred since Harlem was no better and much worse.

"I got a Pro Tools in the bedroom," he said and led the way.

"Pro tool huh?" she asked, assuming he meant his dick. Dudes do call it a tool so if he wanted his to be a pro tool she didn't have a problem with it. She still wasn't sure how far she would go as they headed to the back. They bypassed the master bedroom and entered the spare. Inside was a Mac, and recording equipment.

"I record a lot of my shit right here," he said and booted up the computer.

"Oooh! Pro Tools!" she reeled when the recording software appeared on the screen. Lil Bruh titled his head in confusion, then lit a blunt.

"No thank you," Callie declined when he tried to pass the blunt, then again when he offered to pour her a drink.

"More for me," he shrugged and laughed but must have been serious since he poured a glass of straight liquor. She shrugged it off as well when he handed her the headphones. It only took the cops having to come once, before he accepted getting out of the hood required not living like you were still in the hood. "Go to the mic,"

"OK," Callie agreed and stepped to the microphone setup in the corner. The foam back splash on the walls made a makeshift recording booth. Callie practiced her hook and added to it each time it came around. She enjoyed hearing herself in the earphones but Lil Bruh cut the music off after a few minutes. "Awe man!"

"Check it!" he said, slightly slurred from the weed and liquor. Callie was about to ask, 'check what?', until she heard the play back.

He had recorded a couple of the takes and stacked them. A few turns on a few knobs added some popular effects used on most of the popular music on the radio. She was slightly confused until she realized that was her wailing the hook she wrote.

"That's me!" she cheered and bounded to her feet. This required some dancing as she sang with herself on the track. "Wait til my girls get on this!"

"Mmhm," Lit Bruh agreed and stood. He wobbled slightly but was close enough for Callie to catch him before he fell. There they were standing face to face so it was only right they shared a kiss.

A kiss that traveled out of the room, down the hall and into the master bedroom. Callie sighed mentally when she decided to fuck him. They landed on his bed and kept right on kissing until they kissed out of their clothes.

"OK then," Callie said when she gripped his rock hard erection. She was hoping he would eat her out first like Savage but he was hoping for the same thing as he fondled her vagina.

"Pussy all, good, and wet!" he declared as his finger slid in and out of her. He let out a mighty yawn as he reached for a condom from the bowl of condoms he kept by his bed, but he never made it back.

"Bruh?" Callie asked when he slumped over on top of her. She heard the first of many snores and shook her head. "Bruh..."

Callie climbed from under the man and huffed. She looked for her phone to call an Uber but remembered sitting it on the desk in the next room. Being a female set in so she decided to look around a little bit. First she slipped on the T-shirt he had just taken off and inhaled the pleasant fragrance he wore.

She looked at him to see if he would move as she pulled open the nightstand drawer. He just snored so she began to look around. Voodoo warned her about touching guns since touch leaves touch DNA. She used a pen to push it aside and look at the papers.

"Hmmm?" she wondered when she spotted paperwork with Mike's company logo. "Brick City music recording contract."

Callie scanned through since she didn't know exactly

what she was reading just yet. Her eyes went wide at the hundred thousand dollar advance, but skipped over the recoupment part. Words like, 'three sixty' went over her head but she knew who would know. She made sure not to make a sound as she went to collect her phone.

She took pictures of every page before putting it back. Curiosity caused her to pick up the various receipts she found in the drawer. Most were dated the same day which meant the rapper spent half of his advance in one day.

"Sheesh!" she reeled at the twenty thousand dollar down payment for the new car. Then another twenty went to finance the jewelry he had stripped off. The sixty thousand dollar tab made her shake her head again. Her search made her thirsty so she traveled into the sparse kitchen. The choices were even more scant.

"Beer, beer, malt liquor, oh flat champagne!" she laughed and poured some water from the tap. She made her way back to the spare bedroom to listen to herself again but couldn't figure out how to work the program.

"Hmmm?" she wondered when she picked up his phone. She twisted her lips to help her decide if she should go through it or not. Her head nodded with the decision that she should. She definitely should since Dominique knew about the date before he arrived.

"Shoot!" she fussed when she found it locked. Her shoulders shrugged since she could just unlock it with his face. She pulled up the security but found it was set for his iris. She wouldn't risk waking him up so she abandoned her mission. Instead she curled up into the bed with him. He stirred for a moment before wrapping her up. She was soon sound asleep in his arms.

❄

"Mmmm," Callie moaned when she awoke to the wonderfully familiar feel of a rock hard morning wood pressed against her ass. This was when Voodoo would lift her leg and slide in from behind. Her leg began to lift when she suddenly took notice of another sensation.

"What the..." she wondered and reeled when she realized she was in the middle of a cold, wet puddle. It made her wonder if they already fucked but this was bigger than the wet spot left after some good sex.

"Fuck! My bad," Lil Bruh sighed as he came fully awake himself.

"Your bad what?" she shot back since he seemed to know exactly what was going on.

"Huh? Nah, I just drank too much," he explained but she still had to figure out what that meant. Her mind ran through a medley of memories until she remembered little Stephen. A foster brother she once had who had a bad habit of peeing his bed.

"Eeeewww!" Callie shrieked when she processed that not only had he peed the bed, he peed her as well. She bolted from the bed and into the ensuite bathroom. The water was ice cold since she didn't wait to adjust it until she was already under it.

Lil Bruh just shrugged his shoulders since it wasn't the first time he peed the bed. In fact he peed the bed most nights. He picked up his phone and checked messages and notifications while she scrubbed herself. Callie peeled off her panties and washed them out too since they had been peed on as well. By the time she wrung them out she realized how funny this was and cracked up. Luckily Lil Bruh couldn't hear the laughter from under the spray of water.

"You tryna let a nigga tap that?" he had the audacity to asked when she came back wrapped in a towel. A flurry of curses ran through her mind but she let them all pass before opening her mouth.

"Un-uh, you got me all sore from last night daddy!" she declined.

"I did?" he asked since he couldn't remember. "I 'musta beat that pussy up huh?"

"Did you! My shit throbbing!" she said going for the Oscar. "Go on and get dressed so you can take me home. I need to put some ice on my coochie!"

"Word!" he nodded and mentally patted himself on the back as he headed into the bathroom and under the shower.

Callie started to get dressed but noticed his phone was still open. She hurried and picked it up to pry inside. First stop was his photo gallery where a glut of pussy pics awaited. She had a vagina of her own so she flicked over to the next folder.

'Aye papi! Aye! Aye!' a boricua mami squealed as Lil Bruh laid pipe from behind. Callie muted the speaker and swiped through the rapper running up in a variety of vaginas. Most times raw dog and not pulling out.

"Glad I didn't fuck you," she mumbled as a text came through from, 'Boss man'. She let out a sigh as she contemplated on whether or not she should read it. The sigh was barely past her lips when she tapped the screen and read the message.

'Talk that bitch into signing and I got you ten racks' Mike urged.

"I'm so tired of being a bitch to these niggas!" she fumed. Her anger built as she read the back and forth from last night. She now knew how Dominique knew about their date. The water cut so she closed the phone and pulled her clothes on. Her panties were still damp but didn't matter.

"I beat it up good huh?" Lil Bruh was asking as he came back into the room until he saw the sour look on her face. He must have forgotten or just been used to peeing on people because he asked, "What's wrong?"

"Huh?" she asked and willed herself to pull herself together. Hollywood beckoned because she switched it up as if the director had just yelled, 'action!'. "Just tired. Ready to get some rest."

"Word. Cuz I beat that box like Dougie Fresh!" he laughed and pulled on his clothes and jewelry. She continued her acting until planting a kiss on his cheek when they arrived back at the dorm.

She noticed Penny's car in the parking lot but Zenobia hadn't made it in yet. It was midmorning and she and Young Vaughn were still in bed.

Chapter 7

"Un-huh," Zenobia said through clenched teeth when Vaughn began writhing in pleasure. She applied the twist to her wrist and the rapper sent millions of little rappers spewing into the air.

"Fuck!" he grunted and leaned forward for a kiss. She shoved her tongue inside his mouth and twirled it around while still jacking his dick.

"You really be mad about me fucking a few broads?" he asked like there was nothing wrong with fucking a few broads.

"Naw, because you fucking them instead of me," she replied and laughed. "Shit, you should be mad at your damn self!"

"That's what I love about yo ass," he laughed and rolled off the bed. He had to respect the fact that she wanted exclusivity, but accepted what he could give her.

"Only thing holding us back from being an us, is you my nigga," she sighed. "Either way, I like you and your company. It'll be whatever you want it to be."

"One day I'ma want it to be err thing!" he declared. Everything was a lot so an awkward silence followed.

"Well, right now I'ma need you to be my driver and take me home," she said as began to dress.

"You 'musta forgot you drove?" he reminded and cracked her up. Her laugh was yet another thing he literally loved about the girl. She had a refreshing goofiness about her despite the obvious above average intelligence. She was wife material if he ever matured enough to be husband material. There were miles and miles worth of vaginas stretched out along that path though.

"Oh well, I do need a weed connect tho" she asked determinedly.

"I thought you were the weed connect?" he laughed. Young Vaughn was once the weed connect himself until he got a deal. Ethan made him cut all illegal activities and supplied all the weed he needed, through Penny and the crew.

"We was..." she sighed and told him all about getting put on, then cut off. "All cuz we ain't wanna sign with them!"

"Good! Don't!" he urged. "I tried to school Lil Bruh, but he ain't tryna hear nothing. That's his peeps, but this is business."

"Callie thinks we should go independent?" she asked since she had no clue what it meant.

"You should! Then, when the labels step to you they gotta come correct! That's what I was going to do but Ethan came correct with the bread." he informed. "Not unless you wanna come in under me? I'm finna start a label!"

"Naw, I'm pretty sure my girls ain't tryna sign to my

boyfriend's label!" she shot back. They both grinned goofy grins at the boyfriend label. She wanted to ask how much he got but didn't. "Anyway, we finna record our album on our own. Then see what these folks 'talmbout!"

"Real talk shawty," Vaughn began in a dead serious tone. "Y'all finna be rich!"

"You know, you're really this close to getting some pussy!" she teased, holding her index finger and thumb an inch apart.

"This close," he said and pressed her fingers closer. "Especially since I'm gonna put you on to my old connect."

Zenobia smiled, nodded and moved her finger just a little closer.

"WE'RE GONNA NEED YOU TO PEE ON THIS STICK!" CALLIE blurted as soon as Zenobia opened the door. It was meant to be funny but Penny took it another direction.

"Speaking of pee! Guess who got peed on!" Penny howled. Zenobia didn't have to guess since Penny was pointing at Callie.

"Ion even know if I wanna know what that means!" she said and shook her head.

"Means Lil Bruh pee the bed," she said sorrowfully. She was keeping the part about nearly sleeping with him to herself.

"Y'all fuck?" she wanted to know.

"Eeeww no!" Callie shrieked leaving no doubt of her veracity. Zenobia wasn't done yet though.

"How 'bout you? You fucked Ethan? He looks like one

of them big dick white boys, since he likes rap music," she nodded along with her assumptions.

"No!" she reeled like she hadn't thought about it.

"You know she is the virgin of the crew," Callie said, nodding in appreciation. She was nearly a virgin herself since she decided to remove Savage from her body count. That only left Voodoo and she could live with that. The thought of nearly sleeping with Lil Bruh sent a shiver up her whole soul.

"Ion even want to know what that was!" Penny laughed when Callie shivered and shook.

"Girl..." was all she could say, thinking about all those sex videos. "Niggas need a period too so they can let that dick rest!"

"Um, OK?" Zenobia laughed. She didn't disagree though. She was about to share the good news but Callie jumped back in.

"Anyway, I got dude whole contract!" Callie reported then remembered more news. "Oh yeah! He got a computer thingy in his apartment. I sang on the hook but he want y'all to come in on it too!"

"OK! Bet! Hell yeah! When!" Penny and Zenobia cheered and asked.

"Ion know. I guess he will hit me back," she guessed. Which was one reason she didn't snap on him like she wanted to.

"And, how did you get his contract?" Penny wondered and produced a sample copy of one of Ethan's contracts. The one he brought to the meeting was tailored for them but Mike confiscated it.

"I know how you got that one..." Zenobia said and gave an invisible dick a blow job.

"Gotta work the wrist girl!" Callie cheered her along.

"Shoot, he almost got him some pussy!" Penny declared to her friend's surprise.

"Say whaaaaat!" they both laughed and leaned in for details.

"Almost, we kept it business tho," she said and recalled running up out of the apartment. She nearly went back to Savage's unit on the way down to release that pressure. Until she remembered putting him on blast. Good blast though since the video was getting him a lot of new pussy. Like an eighteen wheeler from the pussy manufacturing company pulled up and unloaded more pussy. And that's quite a bit of pussy.

"Chile, I can't make heads or tails of this shit!" Callie sighed as she looked over the documents while Penny looked at the pictures she took of Lil Bruh's contract.

"Me either, but I know this is bad!" Penny announced when she saw the phrase 360. Then did her best to explain what Ethan explained to her. Which still left more 'splaining to do than Lucy Ricardo.

"We need to talk to a lawyer," Zenobia admitted.

"We can wait a few years until Brandon passes the bar," Callie said, but only because he had just text. They needed a lawyer sooner than that but his law professor just might be able to help.

"I know she is not serious!" Zenobia fussed when she called him back.

"Sup ma! I need to holla at you!" he proclaimed happily. He always sounded like that when he had stacks of cash to give them. Mainly because it meant he had stacks of cash left over for himself.

"Ain't really much to talk about," Callie sighed since they were scraping the bottom of the barrel.

"Ooh!" Zenobia shouted when she remembered the good news she had.

"I'ma holla back yo," Callie said and signed off the call. "Oooh what?"

"Oh, just got us a new plug," she said coyly and pulled her phone to text Young Vaughn.

"Word B?" Penny shot back and got a head shake from Callie. "My bad."

"For real," she laughed as Zenobia and her boyfriend went back and forth.

"Ugh!" Zenobia huffed when she got to a point she didn't like and dialed his line. "Boy we not finna go to some niggas house in Decatur with a rack'talmbout, Vaughn sent us."

"Damn shawty!" Young Vaughn groaned. The girl below looked up with a mouthful of dick to see if he was talking to her.

"Your shawty!" she reminded and paused to see if she actually was or not.

"I'm finna come get you."

he sighed. It wasn't the ride he dreaded but hated abandoning a blow job.

"Thank you baby!" she sang happily and hung up.

"Hole up shawty," he sighed and put the blow job on hold. "Keep that mouth moist until I get back."

"OK," the groupie said like groupies say. He tucked the dick away and headed over to the dorms to pick up the girls.

❄

"He's here," Zenobia relayed when she received Vaughn's text saying just that. They all grabbed a bag containing a third of their re-up money. It probably wouldn't help since they weren't getting on a plane but when plans work, you stick to them.

"Can't wait to see ole girl's face when she finds out we got a new plug!" Callie snarled since Dominique hit her up for dinner as if they were still cool.

"Ion see why she needs to know that?" Penny shot back. She put the question mark in her tone not to sound bossy but it was still some shit a boss would say. That's why Callie's head began to nod in agreement.

"True that," she conceded and gave her some dap. Zenobia missed the whole exchange trying to hurry to her boyfriend.

"I got shotgun!" Penny called when they exited the building. She and Callie cracked up at the puzzled look on her face.

"Girl!" she laughed along with them so Young Vaughn would be met with a cheery face.

"Sup shawty. Sup y'all," he greeted as they all piled in his car.

"Oh hey! We good! Word! Mmhm!" they clowned from the backseat while the couple lip locked and tongue twirled in the front.

"Y'all stupid!" Zenobia laughed when she got her tongue back in her own mouth. Vaughn chuckled as he pulled away from the curb. A phone in the center console began to buzz but Vaughn looked straight ahead as if he didn't hear it. "That's the hoe phone."

"Ooooh!" Penny and Callie laughed some more. They

found plenty more to laugh about as they rode the short journey over to Decatur Georgia.

"Home of the original Dope Boy!" Young Vaughn sighed. Like most males who came up in this city he looked up to the legendary dope boy like a hero. Cameron Forrest was the hoods Hank Aron, Black Panther and Superman all rolled into one.

Penny and Callie ignored the couple up front and watched the scenery change from city to suburb. They exited off Candler road and made a couple turns until they turned into Eastwyck apartments. Vaughn made a call to announce his presence and was meant by a pack of young guns with guns.

"That nigga Young Vaughn!" one of the teens pronounced and proceeded to mob the fledgling super star.

"Sup y'all. Where Ant?" he greeted and dapped everyone of them. The girls took in the lesson of humility and not forgetting where one has come from.

"Right here," his partner said from the doorway. Vaughn excused himself and led the girls inside. All eyes were on their backsides until they entered the apartment.

"This my girl Z. Callie and Penny," he introduced.

"Sup Penny," the dope boy greeted since all he heard and saw was the white girl.

"Sup," she shot back while Callie shook her head, then focused on the personal pile of weed on the table. It was a pretty lime green with colorful hairs. Commonly known as, 'that's that shit'. If that's what he was selling they were in business.

"My peeps need some weight," Vaughn cut in.

"Hell naw shawty!" Ant laughed and shook his head.

"You the first nigga to make it out of here on some legit shit. I ain't finna sell you shit! Fo yo peeps!"

"On God shawty! They got their own shit going on!" he laughed and crossed his heart. Callie took it a step further and produced cash. Her friends followed suit until there was more money than he could ignore.

"Your turn," Penny challenged.

"I like your style," Ant laughed and stood. He took the stairs two at a time and came back that much quicker with a duffle bag. He began placing bricks from the bag onto the table. "My turn huh?"

"I like your style too," Penny smiled when he added an extra pound at the end.

Chapter 8

"*D*ominique here," Callie sighed when she read the text.

"Mmhm," Zenobia hummed sarcastically. "I don't like that bitch tryna divide and conquer us!"

"That bitch can't do either one with me!" she shot back hotly.

"We know!" Penny jumped in before things escalated. She didn't like it either but trusted Callie.

"I'm just saying, let the bitch expose her hand. Then we meet with Ethan and see who is bringing the bag," she explained to Penny, then turned to Zenobia. "Plus the line is gonna be open so you can hear err thang!"

"My bad," Zenobia sighed and twisted her lips. She was really mad that Vaughn was headed to South Carolina for a show. That meant some of that good South Carolinian pussy at the after party, after the show. The girls dapped and hugged like dudes do and Callie headed out the door. She made her way out front where Dominique's Benz was parked and hopped in.

"Gave your car away!" she laughed when she hopped into the passenger seat.

"Yeah," she sighed. Her mouth opened to explain about the blood but remembered what Penny said about not telling her everything. Besides, their weed business was back up and running with no thanks from her.

"So anyway, check this out," Dominique said and pressed the button on her steering wheel. She already cued up what she wanted her to check out so it immediately came out of the speakers.

"That's?" asked and leaned forward to listen closer. It was Lil Bruh's new song plus someone she was vaguely familiar with. "Me!"

"That's you ma! All you!" the woman nodded and smiled with her smiles.

"But wait! My girls were supposed to be on it too!" she protested and pouted. "Supposed to be Lil Bruh featuring the Pretty Thugs!"

"Bitch you the Pretty Thugs! The sooner you realize that, the sooner you get rich! It was Dianna Ross and the Supremes, not just, the Supremes!" Dominique demanded. Callie was at a loss for words but she had more. "You not a Pip, you Gladys!"

"Nah, I'm one third of the Pretty Thugs!" Callie said and lifted her head triumphantly. She even looked up at the passing street sign to figure out where to tell her girls she was so they could pick her up.

There was a moment of silence while Dominique mourned that idea since it was clearly dead. Now she had to tell Mike she struck out. His name was on the company and he had been getting the big head lately. Saying she brought nothing to the table but a fork. She brought the pussy too but he was making it abundantly clear that there was a lot of pussy out there. No, she needed to land Callie or the crew.

"Hmp!" Dominique huffed at the thought that passed through her head. It was an effective one but putting a gun to her head and making her sign could definitely have some legal ramifications.

"Look ma. I appreciate you! I really do. If you ain't put us on with the weed we would be stripping or working at dick in the box," Callie placated since neither option would have been on the table. The Pretty Thugs would rob banks or boost before that happened.

"So you owe," Dominique moaned. Her lip quivered as she contemplated her own future if she didn't get it done. She had no idea what a dick in the box was but was pretty sure she didn't want to find out. She was still plenty fine but thirty five year old strippers don't compete well with eighteen and nineteen year old strippers. Callie looked straight ahead and pretended not to see her knock a tear away. She hit her friends on the speed dial so they could listen in.

"We owe but, we owe ourselves too. We owe it to ourselves to get the best possible deal we can get," Callie insisted.

"Independent is risky," she warned just like Ethan had. For the first time she gave sincere advice about the business.

"Our risk tho. A risk we are willing to take. Everybody takes from me. From all of us! We just tryna win! If you can't understand, or respect that you can pull over and let me out!" she snapped and knocked away her own tears.

"Both chica. I understand and respect it," Dominique sighed and the car went quiet again. She understood, but knew Mike wouldn't.

Dinner turned out to be actually pleasant. The women laughed and talked about everything other than the music and weed businesses. Dominique accepted her failure. It could cost Mike a few million but Lil Bruh would certainly make it up. She would live with it.

"Thanks ma. And, I'm sorry," Callie said as they rode back to her dorm.

"You're welcome and don't be! I still want to help you though. Think about at least letting us, no me, manage you? This is a rough business. You need a rough bitch on your team," Dominique offered. "Don't answer now, just think about it. Talk to your girls."

"I will, I..." Callie was saying until she heard her own voice again. Both women looked at each other, then down at the radio. The song was on the radio.

"The song is on the radio? Come on ma!" Callie snapped. It was bad enough she had to explain it to her girls without it already being on the radio.

"On God Ion know how! Or why!" she insisted and dialed Mike. The call went to voicemail but this wasn't a conversation for voicemail. Callie crossed her arms over her chest which was the universal sign language for, 'I ain't got no talk'. "I'll figure it out. That's my word!"

"What's to figure out! Y'all grimy as fuck!" Callie was convinced. She hopped out before Dominique brought the car to a complete stop in front of her dorm. She only got two steps before Dominique stomped on the pedal and chirped out. Luckily for her most police were busy with black men killing each other because she sped through the city and barely touched the breaks. She ignored all traffic signs and the speed limits as she sped home.

"This nigga got some explaining to do!" Dominique

growled as she stomped into the house and up the stairs. The sounds of sex emanating from the open master bedroom slowed her as she neared. She could only hope it was Mike watching some porn to get worked up for her to come home. It wasn't though and she walked in on Mike with some barely legal teen folded up on their bed.

"Sss, mph, mph, ssss," the eighteen year old hissed and moaned as Mike delivered the dick to her internal organs.

"Why is Lil Bruh song on the radio!" she demanded as she confronted him.

"Huh?" he asked as he processed both her presence and the question. "Shit, I let the DJ hear it and they loved it. Went ahead and ran with it."

"It's not cleared! I couldn't get her to sign!" she said over the splash of the young girl's squishy box. He was still pumping so she was still whining and moaning. Dominique tried to ignore the fact that his dick was stuffed into some teenager on their bed.

"What good are you?" Mike asked and paused his stroke. The girl let out a sigh of relief at the brief reprieve. "Flip over, on your side,"

"I tried to..." Dominique was trying to say as they changed positions. The crack in her heart extended even more when she saw his bare dick dripping with the girl's juices. "You not even strapping up now huh."

"You worried about the wrong, damn thing!" Mike said as he eased back inside the teen. "You need to get them bitches on my roster! Until then, go wash my car."

"Wash your car!" Dominique shot back like she suddenly remembered who she was.

"You ain't good for shit else!"

Mike shot back and dug deeper into the girl.

Dominique squinted to make sure this was the same dude she had been with all these years. It dawned on her that he was. She knew he was fucking a bunch of chicks back in Jersey but ignored it. Her turning a blind eye was the prelude to him fucking them in her face and in her bed. She didn't mean to stand there and watch. It wasn't until he grunted and ejaculated inside of the girl that she snapped out of it. She knew Mike could be evil when he wanted to so she turned and went to wash his car.

"Hey!" he called after her before she could get too far.

"Yes!" she ran back to eagerly accept his apology so she could forgive him for the hundredth time.

"Drop this bitch off on your way to the car wash!" he said and rolled over.

"Mmhm!" both remaining thugs hummed hotly when Callie walked in the room. She already knew what it was about and began to explain.

"Damn Mike!" she shot back since she had already received a gang of congratulatory text messages about the new song on the radio. "Dominique ain't even know he was going to push it out already."

"Without us tho!" Penny fussed and turned to Z.

"Of course you're gonna look out for your lil partner!" Zenobia shot back.

"On God, I ain't know! We a fucking team, I ain't did shit without y'all yet! Matter of fact..." Callie said and pulled her phone. She hit the number and put it on speaker.

"Sup ma! About time you hit a nigga!" Lil Bruh said, smiling through the phone.

"What's up with the song tho! What happened to waiting for my girls?" she demanded hotly. Her word and honor was on the line and she didn't take either one lightly.

"Yo! That nigga Mike ain't even tell me!" he vowed so believably Zenobia's lips untwisted. "Unc be bugging sometime!"

"And got me looking crazy with my girls!" Callie fussed. Now it was her lip that quivered from hurt feelings.

"Have em call me ma. I'll tell them the deal," he vowed. "Oh yeah, I'm performing on Saturday. I want you on stage with me!"

"Bruh, I just told you I ain't doing shit without my girls," Callie said and shook her head.

"Shit bring em! Hell yeah! That's gonna be dope as fuck!" he cheered. "Video too! You know I wanted all y'all on the song!"

"I'll have to see wha..." Callie was saying but Penny and Zenobia beat her to the punch when they leaned in and said, "Hell yeah!"

"Bet that. You gonna let a nigga tap that ass again?" he smiled through the line again.

"Mmhm," Callie laughed and clicked off.

"I thought you said y'all ain't fuck?" Zenobia challenged.

"Which means we didn't. Nigga smoked and drank himself into a coma," she replied. "Plus, Ion know if I was going to give it up anyway!"

"Yeah you are," Penny nodded. Callie scrunched her face to fuss but Zenobia tossed her two cents in as well. "Yeah you are!"

"Y'all buggin!" Callie laughed. "Dude peed the bed!"

"Oh yeah!" Zenobia cracked up. "Vaughn on that same show so we finna be on stage twice!"

"You know what that means!" Penny cheered.

"Yes, we need to shop!" Zenobia cheered.

"I was gonna say we need to get our own songs together! We can eat off their clout forever!" Penny answered.

"Wow! Not you becoming business minded!" Callie reeled.

"Ethan told me a bunch of stuff but, we do need to shop tho!" she cracked up.

Chapter 9

"*S*up Davinci," Savage greeted when the man came to cop a few more pounds. He was quickly becoming his best customer.

"You my dude," he greeted and dapped him up as he entered the unit. "Need a couple more of them thangs!"

"You running through pounds like water! I sold you half my re-up!" he admitted on his way to grab the last of his supply.

"Speaking of re-up, I really be needing more weight?" Davinci put out and titled his head to gauge his reaction. Savage only pondered the query for a second before returning his answer.

"Just let me know what you need, and I'll get it for you," he said, keeping his cut intact. People always asked for his connect to cut out the middle man. But being a middle man kept the rich kid from having to ask his rich parents for anything.

"Check," he sighed and nodded. Not that he necessarily agreed, he was just going to go another route to find his connect. They completed the transaction and traded dope for dollars.

"Umm..." Savage hummed as he scrolled through his phone to decide which thug he wanted to call for his re-up. He has mixed emotions about Penny since she played him, but he did get a truckload of new pussy from the viral video. He conquered Callie which left the door open of hitting it again. Despite her vowing it would never happen again.

"Mmm, mmhm!" he decided when the memory of Zenobia's sweet taste made his mouth water. He licked his vagina licking lips. They weren't as smooth as they usually were.

'Huh?' wondered and ran his tongue back and forth over the bump on his lip. It was definitely there so he headed into the nearest bathroom and looked in what his old grandmother used to call the looking glass. "The fuck is that?"

Savage spent a few minutes investigating the bump on his lip. He decided to seek professional help and grabbed his phone. He headed straight to the Doctorweb.com site to diagnose his damn self. All signs pointed towards one of the popular herpes varieties, but he decided on a regular old pimple. His shoulders shrugged and he resumed his mission.

Zenobia's work phone went straight to her voice mail since she was on her way to meet the stud. Her daddy was moving a steady stream of weed inside the prison. His next call went to Callie but Callie had Brandon driving her around to make her other runs. A heavy sigh preceded his last call to Penny.

"Hey porn star!" Penny laughed when she took his call.

"Whatever. I need another ten," he said.

"Again?" she reeled and furrowed her brow. He was running through pounds like water. So much that he had bought almost half of the last re-up.

"Business is booming," he replied with a shrug she couldn't see.

"I'll be through in a few," she agreed and pulled on her shoes. The order required a stop by the storage unit since they didn't keep anything in the room after the visit from the Dean. "Plenty of time for you to find some pants."

"I..." Savage was saying until he realized he would be saying it to himself. He looked down at the lump in his ubiquitous gray sweats and shrugged again. "She knows she wants this dick."

"Swear everyone wants his damn dick," Penny fumed as she headed down to her car. The girls were minor celebs to some so those sums greeted and spoke every time they came through.

"P-money! Hey Penny!" the girls sang, smiled and cheered. "Pretty thugs! P-money! Cracker!"

"Hey y'all. Sup girl! Look at you all cute! Huh?" Penny was saying until she processed the slander.

"C, r, a, c, k, e, r. Cracker. Cracker ass wanna be black cracker," a dred headed high yellow girl insisted as she came forward.

"Wait, you're not white too?" Penny asked with a straight face. The chick was almost lighter than Zenobia and Zenobia was nearly the same color as Penny.

"Oooh! Ha! Cracked her face!" the other residents cheered and dared. Penny cocked her head to see where she wanted to go with it. The girl flipped her dreds and stormed off. "Thought so!"

Penny's head shook all the way to her car. She got in and pulled out of the parking lot. The dred was posted up with some more of her 'woke' crew pointed as she passed. Penny pointed back with her middle finger and went about her business.

"COME ON IN," SAVAGE GREETED AS HE PULLED THE DOOR open. He basked in glory when he saw Penny's eyes run down his exposed chest, over the ripple of his abs and drop down to the dick. "Mmhm."

"Damn Pepe Le Pew," she fussed and stormed into the apartment. The stacks were stacked up on the table so she made a beeline over to it. She waited until the count reached what it should reach before removing the bricks of compressed weed from the bag. She noticed some movement behind her and turned to see Savage with his dick in his hand. "Bruh!"

"I'm saying, since you, like, to watch so much," he said seductively as he worked up a rock hard erection.

"Go 'head then!" she fussed but she was fronting. She had no interest in him but did like to see dicks.

"You need to, let me suck that pink pussy, while I ssss stroke," he grunted and hissed.

"Mmm, I would..." she moaned and rubbed her crotch through her jeans. "But you got a big ass,bump on your lip!"

"Huh? Oh no, nah that's just, I um, a pimple," he stammered as his erection began to deflate.

"Yeah, I bet," she laughed and stood. Penny headed out the front door while he went to get another look at the bump on his lip. The elevator door opened on the way up and Ethan was inside.

"Hey?" he asked, but quickly remembered this is where he met her. Which reminded him of something else he needed to talk about. Not with the couple riding up with them though so he asked, "Got a sec."

"Sure," Penny agreed and rode up to his floor. He led the way into his apartment and offered a seat and drink. "Sup?"

"You guys are on the verge of becoming rich and famous. Well, rich because you're already famous," he began. The video of the fight in the club already had over a million views.

"We're ready!" Penny cheered and danced in her seat.

"Uh, no you're not," he cut in and cut the music in her head. "First, you have to stop selling weed. It's still not legal. Don't get in trouble and blow it."

"We gotta eat!" she quickly shot back. Ethan just shook his head at the piss poor excuse.

"Looks like you guys are eating pretty good already," he said with a nod at the bag of cash. "Anyway, I heard Callie is signing with Dominique? They put her on a song with Lil Bruh?"

"Fake news!" she shot back and explained how Mike went behind even his own artist. "But he wants us to perform with them this weekend."

"I'm not sure if that's a good idea," Ethan hummed. Penny was about to ask why not since it was more exposure. "Are they paying you? I'm paying you guys to sing with Young Vaughn, is Mike going to pay you?"

"I..." Penny was saying but Ethan had more.

"How much did he pay Callie for the feature?" he challenged.

"Nothing. She didn't even know he was going to use it yet," she shot back.

"Listen. You girls are over your head! The idea of being independent could work, but you still need a manager," he stated plainly.

"So manage us," she offered.

"That's not a decision you can make for the rest," he informed. "Let's meet Sunday for brunch."

"Brunch it is," she agreed and stood to leave. She would have stayed longer if he asked. He didn't so she departed. She had a bag full of money and it was time to go shopping.

"THIS IS EVERYTHING!" ZENOBIA DECLARED AND HELD A leather mini dress up to her frame.

"Not sure if all that ass is gonna fit in that?" Penny wondered as she took it from here and held it against her backside.

"Now, you got a lil 'mo ass than the average white girl but..." Callie laughed since it wasn't as much ass as she was toting around. She took the dress from her and held it against herself. "This works!"

"Now for shoes!" Penny declared and led the way to pick out shoes. Her and Zenobia gushed and fussed over high heels and pumps while Callie had an idea of her own. They didn't notice when she dipped out but certainly took notice when she returned.

"Harlem shit!" Callie insisted and stomped her foot to

show off the wheat colored Timberland boot. Otherwise known as the official footwear of New York City.

"OK, OK!" Penny nodded and reached back onto the shelf. Since they were representing their hood she grabbed a stiletto from the shelf. "Brentwood shit!"

"That really don't, yeah, un-uh," Zenobia declined since Brentwood California isn't exactly a hood. They were on to something though by expressing their individuality. Her head nodded as she walked away and out the store.

"Brentwood shit tho? Don't say that anymore," Callie clowned as they headed to the counter. Penny had paid for her shoes and headed out just as Zenobia returned.

"Atl all day shawty!" Zenobia announced with a Braves hat tilted to the side and a pair of K-Swiss tennis shoes in her bag. All heads nodded as they settled on an image. They would dress similarly but still express where they were from. It sure beats 'bussin it open in a bikini like Lil Kim.

"We need to talk about our own hoods and customs," Callie added as they walked to the food court.

"Fa sho!" Zenobia agreed.

"Yeah cuz I don't know shit about the hood," Penny admitted. Trying to come up with lyrics about what she never experienced sounded forced and unbelievable.

"But you do know about high fashion. First class flights, five star hotels!" Callie shot back. She had more fodder to feed her but her phone buzzed in her purse. Her lips twisted when she pulled it out and saw the name. The eye roll told her friends who it was before she greeted, "Sup Dominique?"

"Where you at?" Dominique asked excitedly.

"Lennox, with my thugs," she informed to represent in case she was on some more divide and conquer shit.

"Stay there! I'll hit when I get there," she said and hung up. Callie fought the urge to leave just because she was told to stay. They were hungry though so they continued on their way to the food court for lunch.

Footwear wasn't the only individuality they expressed since they all shared different taste in food. Callie went for a few slices of pizza while Zenobia wanted wings. Penny came back to the table with some California rolls and spring water.

"So, is Mike going to pay you for the hook?" Penny asked once Callie had a mouthful of sauce and mozzarella.

"Hmp," she hummed and held up a finger while she chewed.

"Cuz, Ethan said you should have gotten writing credits and paid up front," Penny added while Callie worked the food down her throat. "I saw him when I met with that lil hoe, Savage."

"True cuz he said we getting royalties off Young Vaughn song," Zenobia added even though she wasn't exactly sure what or how.

"I came up with the words," Callie agreed and nodded. Her face changed at the thought of being taken advantage of. Then remembered her footwear since she reached down and put the new boots back on.

"Uh-oh! I know that look!" Zenobia laughed and shook her head.

"That look means we're going to jail," Penny sighed. Not that it mattered since she was down with her thugs for whatever.

Whatever came just as they wrapped up their lunch and Dominique texted from the entrance. She specified which entrance and the crew marched off to do battle. Dominique better have something good to say or she was about to get jumped.

"Been played all my life," Callie growled as the memories of foster homes flashed through her head. She wanted to cry but would rather fight instead.

"Where is this bitch at?" Zenobia demanded as they surveyed the parking lot. They all overlooked the black Benz with the red bow since it didn't pertain to them. It didn't until Dominique stepped out smiling and waving them over.

"Over here yo!" she called from behind a pair of large, designer glasses.

"What the..." Callie wondered as she dragged her new boots over to the shiny new car.

"Base model..." Penny mumbled since Penny knew new Benzes better than most.

"Still," Zenobia added since she still wasn't sure what was going on. Neither was Callie so she asked.

"What's going on?"

"You ain't think we weren't going to look out for your contribution to the song!" Dominique reeled like it was the craziest thing in the world. In truth she went out on a limb to make it happen since Mike intended to screw her out totally. Even if the new car was only worth a fraction of what royalties would be on a hit song. Still it was something where Mike wanted to give nothing.

"I'm saying tho?" Callie asked for clarity since foster care taught her to question everything since everything had a motive behind it.

"Bitch this you!" she explained and extended her hand with the key fob.

"Take that shit!" Penny and Zenobia shouted.

"You heard your girls, take it!" Dominique urged. Callie's head lifted with the notion that she did indeed earn it. The song had played again on the way to the mall and would soon be in rotation just like the one they did with Young Vaughn.

"OK," she agreed and plucked the key fog from her hand.

"Now, a bitch needs a ride home!" Dominique laughed.

"Where's Mike?" Penny asked since that was her solution.

"I'll take you," Callie offered since it was only right. "I'll see y'all back at the spot."

"Hurry up yo," Zenobia said, lifting her chin at Dominique defiantly. Dominique stifled a smirk since she had to respect it. She wished she had a few friends like that herself. If wishes counted for something she would wish she could go with them instead of back to the house where she wasn't wanted.

Mike treated her worse by the day since she hadn't delivered the group to his label yet. Now he openly flaunted a parade of young girls around the house. She moved into a spare bedroom after he kicked her out the master. This was her last ditch effort and she bet it all with the car. She used his money so it was her ass if it didn't go down.

"First things, first," Dominique said before Callie could pull away. She opened her designer purse and retrieved a paper. Callie knew exactly what it was since she had recently handed one over to Brandon. "The title to a 2022 Mercedes..."

"Dang!" Callie said, sounding more like Zenobia than herself. The lines between the three blurred everyday as they bonded.

"I know right," Dominique cheered happily. Her face took a serious tone a second later. A second after that she produced a second set of papers from the same purse.

"What's this?" Callie asked despite the title on the document clearly on the top.

"A record contract," she replied just above a whisper. Only because the contract was just a whisper above slavery. The deal shorted them out of everything they had coming.

"I can't," Callie sighed and shook her head.

"I don't blame you. It's a shitty deal," she admitted and pulled off her shades. Her eye was swollen and purple on its way to turning black. The sight knocked the wind out of Callie like a punch to the gut.

"He did that to you?" she growled like she was ready to do something about it.

"Yeah after I beat up some young bitch he had in our room. I ain't care about him fucking the bitch, but why the bitch wearing my clothes!"

"So, what's going to happen now?" Callie wondered.

"Not sure. I still have Lil Bruh signed under me as his manager. I'll still eat," she declared.

"We'll figure something out. I'll drop you off and see you at the show," Callie sighed and pulled away.

Chapter 10

"*I*'m going to ride over to Vaughn's. I'll just meet you guys at the club?" Zenobia put out to see what she got back.

"Cool but, what's in the bag?" Callie challenged.

"Prolly same thing that's in your bag!" Penny pointed out since Callie had packed an overnight bag as well.

"Nah cuz we, I be, supposed to be," Callie stammered, stuttered and came clean. "Man, I need some dick!"

"Me too," Zenobia admitted. She didn't like that Young Vaughn had hoes but did like him. What she wasn't going to do was let them hoes get all the dick while she got none.

"Me three except, not!" Penny laughed. She was still laughing when her friends left with their bags. Laughed as she watched them drive away from the parking lot. Then let out a sinister laugh when she dug up her Rose. "Bwahahaha!"

All three girls were a little nervous about this bigger show in the bigger venue. Zenobia and Callie were going to party with their little boyfriends. Probably have a drink, smoke a little weed. That wasn't an option for Penny so she was going to bust a good nut.

Her outfit for the show was neatly laid out on the extra bed. Her hair was done and wrapped to withstand the steam of the shower. There was only one thing left to do so she peeled off her pants and panties. Unhooked her bra and lay naked on the bed.

The flower design came to life with a gentle buzz when she turned the knob. She gave herself some foreplay by rubbing the device over her swollen nipples. Slowly down her hard stomach, then around the inside of her legs. The buildup was so intense her back arched completely off the bed when it reached her vagina.

"Sssss!" she hissed and held it down. Not a full minute later she began feeling the flutters throughout her body. She couldn't believe an orgasm had rushed up that quickly. "Nuh-uh!"

It was all 'Un-huh' when she began to writhe and squirm from busting an intense nut. A small puddle formed under her from the excess juice of her juice box. As tight and wet as it was she had some one minute nuts in her future whenever she did give it up. Which could very well be sooner than later.

"Shit! Whew! Damn!" Penny fussed and cussed from the good nut. "Shoot, I may need some dick too!"

Penny didn't pout for too long since the device was still buzzing pretty strong. She didn't want to let the good batteries go to waste so she pressed the pedals against her pussy and went for round two. By the time she reached the shower her legs were wobbly and rubbery from round six.

❄

"GOT A MILLION NIGGAS OVER HERE!" CALLIE FUSSED WHEN she reached Lil Bruh's building. The parking lot was packed with cars so she had to park on the street. She grabbed the overnight bag, then put it back down since none of them niggas needed to know her business.

"Here goes my shorty!" Lil Bruh announced when he opened the door.

"What you got going on?" she immediately wondered when she saw the machine pistol in his hand. She remembered Voodoo leaving the apartment with one, one night, and coming home without it. She found out the rest of that story on the morning news.

"Just chilling!" he said and stepped aside so she could enter. She saw quite a few of his crew had guns but they were just flexing for photos for social media. Real killers never take pictures like that so she relaxed a little. Just a little because some of the girls were fondling the guns too. She knew enough about guns to know they were an accident waiting to happen.

"Y'all goofy bitches need to put them shits down!" she barked. The aggressive tone and slanderous term stopped time. The girls weren't sure how to feel until the host spoke up.

"Y'all heard my queen!" Lil Bruh cosigned. He turned to his right hand man and told him, "Put them shits in the trunk."

"You bringing burners to the show?" Callie asked in confusion. Which wasn't often since she was a pretty smart chick and could usually make sense out of most things. Bringing guns to a show wasn't one of those things.

"Hell yeah! In case we have beef," he said like a hood nigga instead of a black man on the door step of riches.

"Them niggas say anything and it's up!" one of his crew slurred.

"You tryna hit this?" Lil Bruh asked and extended the blunt to Callie. She placed her lips on the tip and locked eyes with him as she took a pull.

"I'm good," she purred with smoke billowing from her nostrils. The single drag was enough to calm her nerves. They continued to party until it was time to go. Callie drove her own car since she was the only sober one in the house. Lil Bruh rode with her since he planned to come back home with her.

"WE'RE GONNA MISS THE SHOW..." ZENOBIA WARNED WHEN Young Vaughn reached between her legs.

"Sho nuff?" he reeled when he caught her meaning. The thought of skipping the show quickly flashed through his mind.

"Un-uh!" she laughed and pushed him up. She was on his team and wouldn't let him miss his money for some pussy. Besides, they would have all night after the show .

"Yeah, let's do this shit. Y'all still on stage with Bruh?" he asked as he put his chains back around his neck.

"Not unless his people come with some bread!" she shot back.

"Ethan took care of y'all right?" Vaughn asked full of concern. He was ready to pull some cash from his own pocket to make sure they were compensated.

"Yeah, we meeting with him tomorrow," she said appreciatively. He was already getting some pussy but the sentiment had her trying to remember the wrist twist Penny spoke of.

"What the hell?" Vaughn laughed at the faraway look in her eyes. She quickly shook it off and laughed with him. "So, y'all finna sign?"

"Naw..." she strained since she wasn't exactly sure what they were going to do.

"Well, let's go turn this shit out!" Young Vaughn said like Young Vaughn says. A smile spread on her face as he transformed from the sweetheart she knew better than most into the star he was on his way to becoming.

Vaughn was a born and bred street dude but picked things up quickly. He held the door open for his lady when they reached the car and waited until she was seated before closing it. She reached over to unlock his side to show she wasn't a selfish bitch like Sonny said in the movie A Bronx Tale, but he used the fob and beat her to it.

"Punk!" she fussed and popped his arm, ruining her recreation of the iconic scene. He was still laughing when they pulled out of the driveway.

The banter and laughter bounced around the car like a pinball as they headed downtown to the venue. A surreal moment swept through the car when the marquee came into view. It was almost overwhelming and Vaughn had to pull over to process it.

"That shit crazy shawty!" he vowed and read his name in lights once more.

"Appearing tonight, Young Vaughn!" Zenobia read with all the fanfare he deserved. There was more so she kept reading the smaller words, "Also performing, Lil Bruh, Skeeter and the Pretty Thugs! OMG!"

She wasn't the only thug reading the sign to her boyfriend though.

"Look yo!" Callie pointed and read, "Also performing, Lil Bruh! And the Pretty Thugs! That's right!"

"How they got that fuck nigga name bigger than mine?" he snarled.

"Huh?" she asked since that made no sense on several levels. First because this was Ethan's show for his artist. It was a courtesy to let Mike's artist open since they were using his facilities to record. The studio fees would finance a whole other project.

Then because Young Vaughn had been out a full month before Lil Bruh dropped. The song was in heavy rotation on the radio, and had been added to stations all over the country. It was number one on the countdown while Lil Bruh was just starting to get spins. She assumed he was joking and laughed out loud.

"Real spit ma, shit ain't funny!" he barked. Callie did a double take and nearly snapped. Then recalled how men could be big babies with huge egos. Voodoo sure threw his share of tantrums.

"It's all good Papi. You got next!" she declared to his delight, then upped the ante. "Shit, you got now! Let's go turn this shit out!"

"WHEW!" PENNY SAID WHEN SHE STEPPED OUT OF THE CAR and wobbled. Her legs were still a bit rubbery from the multiple orgasm.

"You OK?" the valet attendant asked as he caught her.

"Mmhm!" she vowed and headed for the entrance. She cast a glance down the block at the long line, then up at the marquee.

"Can I help you white girl?" the burly bouncer boomed down at her while she was still looking up at the sign. He flexed his pectoral muscles and made his tight shirt dance when she looked down.

"Sure. By stepping your big fine ass to the side so P-money can come in!" she demanded like a diva.

"Check," he nodded and smiled at the compliment as he stepped aside. She added to the group text they maintained to announce their presence. The girls hollered back and told her to come to the VIP section.

"VIP section," Penny said out loud to process it. She had been first class and VIP her whole life but that was on her daddy's dime. This one was all her, and it was just the beginning. Her head turned both ways when she entered the party within the party of the VIP section.

There was a separate party at each table so any table would have done. Callie was with Lil Bruh and his crew while Zenobia was sitting on Young Vaughn's lap. She made one more head turn and saw Ethan and some of his staff holding down a table filled with champagne but there was more talking than bottle popping over there.

"Here she is!" Ethan cheered and cheesed when she arrived at the table. He may not not have been drinking at the moment but wore the happy grin of someone with a nice buzz. He stood and held his arms open for her.

"Hey Ethan," she sang as she took him up on the hug. Her legs wobbled again but this time it was from the touch of a man.

"You OK? Nervous!" he asked and answered when he felt her tremble in the embrace. "Don't be! You're a natural"

"You are!" Jovita seconded. The pretty, black woman looked at least a decade younger than her thirty five years but was Ethan's second in command. She ran most of the day to day operations while Ethan forged the relationships and wrote the checks.

"I'll be fine," she assured them because of all the things Penelope Manning had been in life, nervous was not one of them.

"So, I hear you coming aboard!" Mike cheered and lifted his champagne flute. All of the followers and flunkies all followed suit.

"Huh?" Callie asked. One look Dominique's way said whatever he was talking about was news to her too.

"New Benz is the huh!" he shot back like he was ready to snap. His head snapped in Dominique's direction for clarity. "I know we ain't buy a new car for nothing?"

"Not for nothing. We'll talk when we get home," Dominique urged and looked at the others around the table. Mike had individually screwed them out in different ways so it probably wasn't best to talk details in front of them. That's why they all zoomed in on Mike to see what he would reveal. A few of them received cars as well minus the titles since they had Mike's name on them.

"As soon as we get home," he growled.

"My girls want to get paid to come on stage with us," Callie announced. She wanted to get paid too so she lumped herself in with them.

"They not on the song. Just you," he said and tossed a wad of cash across the table. Callie was on the verge of walking off and leaving the money on the table. She looked at Dominique who pleaded with her eyes. The fear was clear but Callie didn't know enough about Mike to be afraid of him.

A smirk spread on Callie's face as she reached for the money. Mike basked in the satisfaction of his plans to divide and conquer. Callie was the clear leader so if he bagged her, the others had to follow. Callie felt all eyes on her as she got up and walked over to where Young Vaughn was holding court with his counsel. Zenobia saw her coming and got up off his lap to meet her. Penny excused herself and walked over as well. That meant all eyes from all three tables were on them.

"Sup?" Penny asked when they were assembled.

"Nothing. Mike just wants me on stage with Lil Bruh," she offered and waited for feedback.

"Do that shit!" Zenobia urged. Penny nodded along and added, "You better kill that shit! You represent us!"

"Pretty Thug shit!" Callie laughed out loud as she began to split the money equally between her crew. A not so subtle snub at Mike and proof he could neither divide nor conquer the Pretty Thugs.

Chapter 11

"I want that car back!" Mike growled in Dominique's ear when he watched Callie split his money. Lil Bruh looked especially confused since he didn't even get paid for the show. His 360 deal ensured that the label ate off everything he did.

"OK," Dominique agreed even though she gave Callie the title. She was determined to do right by the girl even if he shitted on all the other artist. They all realized then he could take their gifts away as well.

"I took a shit load of money from the distributor on the strength of signing the Pretty Thugs," he whispered. It looked like a touching moment between a man and his woman but only because they couldn't hear the malice in his tone. "I better get me some Pretty Thugs."

"OK," she agreed again so he wouldn't spazz out right then. She got a reprieve when Lil Bruh was announced to the stage.

"You better kill that shit!" Mike barked.

"Word!" Lil Bruh assured him. He took it as encouragement instead of the threat it was.

"Do ya thang mama!" Zenobia urged when it was time to hit the stage. She joined Lil Bruh and they went out and killed it.

Callie proved all thoughts right about her. She carried herself like a star. Sexy without having to twerk or degrade herself. The DJ even cut the music and let her blow acapella and the crowd went nuts. Dominique clapped and cheered until she felt the heat on the side of her face. She turned to see Mike looking at her like a demon. Her first instinct was to run. Get up, leave and never come back.

"Yeah! Y'all like that shit! Lil Bruh, C-money in this bitch!" Lil Bruh dared and the audience ate it up. "Y'all may as well go home now! Ain't nothing after this!"

"The fuck he say?" Young Vaughn asked, looking around his table. He figured he misunderstood but the shocked looks on faces told him otherwise.

"That nigga tripping shawty!" Vaughn's partner Cool said, looking confused since they were all cool just a week ago. That's the thing about fame, it's going to go to the head. That's a fact, the only difference was how it would manifest when it did.

"Shit!" Ethan groaned when he heard the slight. The last thing he wanted was rap beef to distract his artist. He looked over at Mike as a cue to control it but it was crystal clear he was loving it.

"The show ain't quite over so don't go no where!" the DJ announced with a chuckle. "Next up, Young Vaughn!"

"Don't worry. It's all good," Penny assured Ethan and began to extricate herself from the packed booth so she could perform. On a last second whim she popped a kiss on Ethan's lips on her way to the stage.

"Oh?" Jovita asked curiously. She and Ethan had a thing slightly less than a fling when she first came onboard. They kept it strictly business after that since business and pleasure rarely mix. Ethan could only shrug since he didn't have an answer.

"The fuck was that about?" Vaughn asked Lil Bruh as they passed each other.

"It's whatever with me nigga!" Lil Bruh declared. Cool stepped up to pop it off since that's what he was there for.

"We want smoke!" one of Lil Bruh's team declared but security stepped in before the smoke could fill the room. Mike looked disappointed since his plan to keep the star of the show off the stage failed. The slight dust up was caught on several phone cameras and was well on its way to becoming viral.

"The show finna start now!" Young Vaughn announced when he took the stage. He launched into his next single to whip the crowd into a frenzy. Once he had them where he wanted them he took it there. "Where my thugs at?"

"Right here daddy!" Zenobia purred into her cordless mic as she led the Pretty Thugs onto the stage. She made sure the world knew they were together by sticking her tongue down his throat onstage, for the world to see.

"P-money in this bitch! C-money back for more!" the other thugs proclaimed. The song came on and got ripped to shreds. The film crew got great footage since this would be added to the upcoming video shoot.

Young Vaughn did what he came to do and slammed the mic once he was done to symbolically say, 'now the show is over'. Ethan just shook his head since he would get the bill for the mic. Jovita patted his hand to let him know it was worth it.

"Y'all need to handle yo biz," Mike suggested to Lil Bruh when the show ended. He said what he said and stood. He pointed at two of the groupies grouped at the table and they stood as well. "Drive us home Dominique."

Callie wanted to protest but Dominique shook her head. Her heart broke for her as she trailed behind her boyfriend and the groupies. She was forced to drive her man home to be cheated on. Her attention shifted to Lil Bruh and his crew as they mounted up.

"Great job! Great footage!" Ethan reported when Penny arrived back at the table. Penny was all smiles until the VIP erupted in violence.

The two groups collided in the middle of the VIP section and slugged it out. Luckily neither side had weapons so they were forced to duke it out like men used to do. Like Craig's daddy said, 'you win some, you lose some, but you live. You live to fight another day'.

Security had a gun though and he wasn't about to try to break up the twenty plus men from fighting. Instead he pulled his gun and fired a shot into the ceiling. The plan was to stop the fight but it was a dumb ass plan. It stopped the fight alright but started a stampede.

"They shooting!" people screamed and ran for their lives.

"Come on!" Ethan shouted and literally picked Penny up and put her on his broad shoulders. He held an arm out like a running back going up the middle and stiff armed his way out of the club. A block later he put her down and opened his car door.

"OK then!" Penny cooed, feeling all protected and

whatnot. If she didn't know any better she might have been turned on. Then again it could have been the after effects of the Rose. She was going to use it again as soon as she got in.

"You OK?" Ethan asked and scrunched his face at the amused look on her face.

"Huh? Yeah!" she said and shook it off. She was only one third OK so she quickly pulled her phone to check on the other two thirds.

"Yoooo!" Callie answered as she sped away from the club. Lil Bruh was next to her holding his shirt to the cut over his eye. "Where you at?"

"With Ethan. Where is Z?" she replied just as Zenobia appeared on her screen. She pressed her name to add her to the call. At the same time Ethan called to check on his multi million dollar investment. He was relieved that Young Vaughn was fine.

"Where y'all at!" Zenobia asked while Young Vaughn drove towards his house. They all reported in that they were fine and agreed to meet at the room. Neither said exactly when before they got off the line.

"We will wait a couple hours before we go back for your car," Ethan said and he steered towards his own building.

"K," she agreed since he didn't ask. He was a boss and sent another tingle in her lady parts.

There was an uncomfortable moment when they reached the building and saw Savage arriving with one of his lady friends. He lifted his chin like he didn't know her, which was fine by her. Not that she could leave it alone though.

"Excuse me, sir?" Penny asked once they were all inside the elevator.

"Me?" Savage asked even though it was clear to the other two passengers who she meant.

"Yes sir. You just have a thing, there, on your lip," she pointed out and turned away.

Savage and the chick had both decided to pretend it wasn't there so they ignored her and looked straight ahead. Ethan couldn't help but to laugh. The stress of the night made it that much more funny and his loud laughter reverberated around the small space. Savage and the woman were both relieved when the door opened. They rushed down the hall to escape the laughter.

"Whew! I needed that," Ethan sighed as they headed down the hall. He was still all chuckles as he opened the door to let them in. Penny on the other hand was all business.

"Where's your room?" she asked. Ethan looked confused by the question but knew the answer.

"Last room, on the right," he said and watched as she walked down the hall and into his room. He shrugged and took a seat on the sofa and waited for her to return. When she didn't he got up to investigate why. He got his answer when he saw her clothes on the floor. Which explained why she was nearly naked on his bed. "Penny I..."

"Please don't say anything and screw it up!" she demanded so urgently he complied. He kicked his shoes off on his way over and joined her on the bed. His tongue slid easily into her mouth and stifled their mutual moans.

His dick was soon so hard it was uncomfortable in his pants. Penny heard the zipper come down and took her tongue back so she could watch. She smiled when the nice, thick erection joined them on the bed. She jumped up and helped out by grabbing his pants by the bottom and snatching them off.

"Alrighty then," Ethan laughed but when she wrapped her lips around the tip of that dick there was nothing else to laugh about.

"Mmhm!" Penny hummed when he flipped her around into the top half of a 69. She slowly lowered her juice box on his thin lips. The suction felt great and got greater when he jetted his tongue inside of her. She rode it like a dick while working her lips and wrist.

"Mmmmmm!" Ethan groaned loudly from under the vagina in his mouth. He was a true gentleman and alerted her to the impending eruption. She heeded the warning and removed him from her mouth. The twist of her wrist was no less pressure and soon his feet twitched under him.

"Pretty much!" Penny laughed when he sent an arch of semen sailing in the air. She stroked him dry and he concentrated his full attention in her sweet pussy.

"Come here," Ethan directed and flipped her onto her back. He took an ankle in each hand and lifted her legs high and wide. Then dove tongue first back into her box. Penny began to squirm and writhe under the twirling tongue. Penny wasn't a gentleman though and gave no warning when she came all in his grill.

"Mmmmm," Penny moaned when he made his way up and kissed her lips. She tasted her own juices on his mouth as they made out. Then felt him rubbing his erection between her vaginal lips. "Wait!"

"I wasn't going to put it in without it," he declared and reached for the nightstand. Penny watched as he opened the condom and rolled his down his dick.

She was waiting for a good time to tell him about the

virginity she wasn't losing tonight. It would have been a great time when he rubbed his dick against those slippery lips once more. Or when he parted them as he eased inside of her.

An, 'owe' escaped her mouth when she felt the sting of womanhood. It mixed perfectly with the pleasure and curiosity. She hissed and winced as he sank further inside of her.

"Damn Penny?" Ethan wondered as he inched further inside. He could only get half way inside and made short, soft strokes. Not many of them though because that brand new vagina quickly got the best of him. He blamed her when he went stiff and filled the condom. "Damn Penny!"

"Damn," she agreed as she accepted what just happened.

"Shit!" Ethan fussed for the same reason. It was never good to mix business with pleasure so he had no intentions on this happening. It happened though. "I'll get us a washcloth."

"For? Oh oK," Penny played it off. Except she winced and hissed even louder when he extracted himself from inside of her.

'Sheesh!' Ethan was thinking as he entered the bath-room. That was the bestest, wettest pussy he had in a long time. He squinted to reflect back to when as he reached the toilet to remove the condom. He let out a slight laugh at the ludicrous rumor of Drake putting hot sauce in a condom. Like, why the fuck would he do that in a bathroom instead of just flushing it down the toilet. Anyway, that's when he saw the blood.

"What the? Holy fuck!" he reeled when he put it

together. Never in a million years would he have suspected the wild child was a virgin. "Oh wow!"

"I know right," Penny laughed when he came back out with a soapy washcloth. She heard the outburst and matched it with the blood on the sheets she was pulling off the bed.

"Why didn't you tell me?" he asked and felt silly for asking.

"Old news," she shrugged and helped him make the bed back. The car would wait until the morning because they climbed back on the bed and cuddled until sleep came.

Chapter 12

*C*allie stole glances at Lil Bruh as she drove back to his house. He was steady sipping and smoking without a care in the world.

The cut over his eye had stopped leaking from the pressure he applied. She nearly blew through a red light for looking at him.

"What's up ma?" Lil Bruh laughed as she skidded to a stop that saved them from cross traffic.

"I'm saying yo," she sighed. Her head shook and she came out with it. "What was that about?"

"What?" he asked so innocently she wondered if he could actually forget the chaos of just a few minutes ago. He didn't, he just thrived on chaos so it was normal to him.

"The fight? You and dude was cool," she reminded.

"We was!" Lil Bruh shot back like a reason was to follow. None did because he didn't have one. Except a good healthy dose of hate for the next man's accomplishments. Not to mention, Mike urged him on since some dumb ass consumers loved beef.

"Yeah, OK," she said and said nothing else until they got to his spot. She seriously considered leaving and going back to the dorm. She didn't though, and grabbed her overnight bag since morning wasn't very far off. Lil Bruh wobbled up to the front door and struggled to get the key into the lock. She had to take it from him to let them both in. "Hope that ain't a sign..."

"Wanna smoke a blunt?" he asked when he saw the pile of fluffy, green buds on the coffee table. Most of his advance went to frivolous shit like weed and jewelry. It should have been twice as weed on the table but each one of those groupies made sure to grab a handful before they left.

"Where are you tryna go B? Mars?" she asked since he was already higher than the moon. The question seemed to only confuse him even more though. Once again she took control. "We're going to bed!"

"Hell yeah!" he cheered and gripped her ass as he followed her to his bedroom.

Lil Bruh wasted no time getting undressed when they arrived. Callie took her time coming out of her clothes and carefully laid them on a chair. She sped up a little bit when she saw the dick. It was a nice height and weight as it stood straight out.

"You got condoms?" she asked and confused him some more. Luckily she brought her own in the bag.

Lil Bruh laid on his back as she joined him on the bed. He reached for her head to pull it down but got it knocked away. If she wasn't doing this for herself he would have been out of luck. His dick throbbed in her hand as she rolled the condom on it. She was already good and gushy from her bout of abstinence.

"Better not come quick!" she warned as she climbed on top of him. She was far too horny to leave things to chance so she took control.

"I'ma beat it up like last time!" he declared while she reached down and worked him inside of her. Lil Bruh believed he knocked it out of the park so much he told Mike how good the pussy was. Mike had all three of the thugs on his list but Callie was first.

"Mmhm," she hummed and twisted her lips sarcastically. They immediately untwisted once she got some dick in her. "Mmmm!"

"Mmmm, is, right, I'm," Lil Bruh was saying with each upthrust of his hips.

"No! I'ma need you to be quiet and, don't, move!" Callie demanded and worked her hips in a semi circle and back around the other way. She added a back and forth rock and he was cool with it.

Only one thing was missing so she closed her eyes and welcomed Voodoo back into her life. She transformed back to that Harlem tenement building with her beloved. Luckily Lil Bruh remained quiet and didn't fuck up her fantasy. Instead the squishy sounds of her juicy vagina filled the otherwise quiet room. Until it wasn't quiet anymore.

"Huh?" Callie asked when she heard a strange sound. Her eyes popped open to look around but all she had to do was look down. Her hips came to a screeching halt when she realized the sound was his snores. Lil Bruh was sound asleep. His dick was still hard so she began rocking, winding and grinding on the dick.

"Nah nigga, I'ma fuck, the shit, 'outa you!" she snarled and worked her hips.

She did too and bust a pretty impressive nut. What was

even more impressive was that Lil Bruh was still hard. She shook and shivered off the first orgasm and went for a second. The second did the trick and she fell off and laid next to him. Callie pulled his T-shirt on to inhale the Killa cologne he wore.

He stirred enough to wrap her up so she could fall asleep in his arms. Morning wasn't far off so she embraced the deep sleep that engulfed her.

The sun rose and peeped through the blinds as phones began to buzz and vibrate. It wasn't those distractions that pulled Callie from her comfortable sleep though.

"Huh?" she asked about the strange sensation. It was almost comfortable until it got cold. She spun and saw Lil Bruh had peed the bed again. "Bruh!"

"My bad," he shrugged and rolled off the bed. She was surprised he had anything left when he went into the bathroom to pee some more.

Callie stripped off the wet T-shirt and rushed into the hall bathroom with her bag. She cursed the whole time she washed and scrubbed the pee from her body. Lil Bruh was still in the bathroom when she pulled her clothes on and fled his house for the last time.

ZENOBIA FARED A LOT BETTER WHEN THEY FLED THE chaotic club fiasco. Young Vaughn still opened her door and let her get seated before getting behind the wheel. People were still in a frenzy from the gunshot but he was calm.

"Ion know what that was all about?" he wondered and

went silent. He strained his brain to figure out what happened between him and Lil Bruh that led to gunshots.

"Jealousy. Plain ole, old fashioned hate," she explained.

The car went silent as they pondered the future. How much more hate would manifest as they became successful. The silence carried them all the way back to his house and into his bedroom. By now Zenobia had her own side of the bed so she headed around and began coming out of her clothes.

Young Vaughn would take her side of the bed when he entertained other females but that was slowing down as of late. Especially since Zenobia figured out how to please him without letting him inside of her. He was so busy in the studio trying to finish up his album there wasn't much time for much else. Whatever time he had he spent with her.

They rolled under the comforter like a married couple and met in the middle of the bed. Lips met then tongues as hands gripped and groped. Zenobia spread her legs wide to let Vaughn freely fuck her with his fingers.

"Sho nuff?" he asked seriously when she gripped his finger so firmly he couldn't move it. She let up with a giggle and let him slip and slide in and out of her. Shit got serious when her hisses and moans got louder and longer.

"Can't, sssstand you!" she hissed and came all over his finger.

"I know right," Vaughn laughed and sucked the nectar from his fingers. Zenobia stared up at the ceiling for a moment. She sighed when she made her decision and pulled him on top of her. It was she who reached down and lined his dick up in between the slippery lips. All he had to do now was push. "You sure?"

"Boy if you don't fuck me!" she fussed and got fucked.

Vaughn worked himself in and around until found a good stroke. He planned to rock her world but it had been many years since he had been inside a woman raw. The witness and tightness had other plans for his night.

"Hold up shawty," he pleaded for a pause but Zenobia wasn't having it. She gripped that dick, wiggled her hips, and that was all she wrote. "Fuck!"

"I know, right," she quipped back with a giggle as he seized as if hit by electricity. He gasped for air and slobbered on her neck while she squeezed and released, squeeze and release. She patted his back and said, "There, there baby. Get some rest."

The couple fell asleep wrapped in each other's arms like a couple should.

MIKE AND DOMINIQUE HAD AN ADVENTUROUS NIGHT themselves. Dominique looked straight ahead as she drove and tried to ignore the action in the backseat. Mike had no intentions of letting her. He and the two girls moaned and groaned louder than necessary.

"Hold up..." Mike declared and leaned back to get the dick out. The girls bumped heads trying to reach it first. "Un-uh, y'all share that."

Dominique gritted her teeth and contemplated running the car into an embankment. That would kill her too and that wouldn't do at all. Instead she lifted her chin and accepted the last straw and final insult. She didn't mind what was going on in the back seat one bit because she was done. The woman was fed up and there was nothing he could do about it. She was running out of love and it was too late to talk about it.

"Come on up to my room," Mike directed once they reached the house. Dominique had already moved to a guest room so she headed there. "You too bitch. We need to talk!"

The most defiance Dominique could muster was blowing her breath hard. The girls laughed and mocked by blowing their breath as well. The trio all began to strip as soon as they walked into the master bedroom. Mike made her attend but couldn't make her watch. She went over to the window and looked down at the pool. It was why she picked this house and would be the only thing she missed.

Still, she couldn't help not to periodically peep back to match the sounds to a sight. The first was both girls going down on him. She turned back another time to see one riding his dick while the other rode his face. Her head shook when she saw he was once again having unprotected sex with strangers. It sent a chill up her spine and put a look of disgust on her face. She made a mental note to get tested for the whole gamut of STDs ASAP.

"Fuck!" Mike grunted and bust a nut in one of the girls. That absolutely astonished Dominique to words.

"You bugging the fuck out!" she vowed. Just as quickly she remembered it wasn't her concern. "What did you wantto talk about?"

"Why did you give that bitch a whip without her signing on the line?" he wanted to know.

"Just because she hasn't signed doesn't mean she won't!" she shot back. "These street, bully tactics ain't gonna fly in business."

"The fuck they ain't! Take that car back and tell that

bitch she won't see a cent from royalties until she is under contract!" he demanded.

"No can do. I gave her the title. You not shitting on her like you did Lil Bruh and the rest," she said. The hurt expression of his face tickled her inside but it didn't last long.

"This bitch thinks this is a game," he told his company. "Y'all beat her ass!"

"I wish these young bitches would try!" Dominique demanded and got her wish.

The slay queens rushed over, slapping and scratching and quickly got papped out. Dominique took her frustrations out on the girls through a series of hooks and haymakers. It wasn't long until they ran right back to Mike and took refuge under the comforter. Now their eyebrows and eyelashes were lopsided from the knots and bumps she put on their heads.

"Now nigga, I'm done!" she shouted. "Fuck you and your company!"

"Tell you what," Mike boomed as he got off the bed. "You're gonna sign over them management contracts too!"

"I'm not signing over shit!" she yelled up into his face. She only caught a glimpse of the speeding right hook that turned off the lights quicker than Teddy Pendergrass.

Chapter 13

"Not cool being late to my own meeting," Ethan sighed as he drove Penny to pick up her car from the club the next day after the chaotic night.

"We could have pulled up together," she offered and cracked up at the look on his face.

"Yeah, no we can't do that," he stated, then took it further. "We can't do this anymore. It's just business or just pleasure."

"No," Penny shrugged and took in the scenery passing by the window. Ethan looked over at her and wondered if she understood what he meant. He sure said it plainly enough and she was definitely smart enough to understand.

What Ethan understood was P-money was a star. The Pretty Thugs would sell millions of records and become rich and famous. She would move on to a solo career and climb even higher. Solo albums, movies, endorsements, merchandise. That was more important than the sex.

"No? What do you mean, no?" he asked, then once again explained his position. "Penny, you need a good manager to take you where you're destined to go. Plus distribution. It's business, not pleasure."

"No. I want you to manage me. I know that part. As far as distribution goes, me and my girls will decide that," she said since they already decided to go with the highest bidder. "But, to deflower me and say we're going to keep it strictly business? Un-uh, nope. You got yourself a whole girlfriend my nigga."

"I, you, I mean..." Ethan stammered, stuttered and sighed in defeat. "My nigga tho?"

The laughter subsided when Penny reached her car. They made out a little before separating for as long as it took to get to brunch. Penny felt alone the second she left so she called her crew.

"Girl," Callie said, shaking her head as she drove to the hotel where they were meeting.

"That good or that bad?" she laughed at her exasperation.

"I'll tell y'all all about it. Finna pull up now," she said.

"Finna huh?" Penny laughed.

"Damn Z rubbing off on me!" Callie cackled. She must have talked her up because Zenobia's name popped on her screen. She quickly added her to the call. "Yoooo!"

"I'm almost there!" Zenobia said as she pulled off the highway.

"Me too," Penny announced. A few minutes later they were all in the parking lot since Ethan went in ahead.

"Yo that shit was cray-cray last night!" Penny declared.

"Word," Callie agreed and shook her head. There was plenty to talk about from the long night but this wasn't the time to talk about it. "Let's handle our business!"

"I'm ready!" Zenobia added. They turned to go inside and turned heads with every step.

"There they are!" Ethan announced and stood from the table. Jovita was there with him and stood as well.

"Hey Ethan," Callie greeted and accepted the first hug. Zenobia was next, followed by Penny.

"Let's get some food and chop it up," he said and led the way over to the expansive buffet. Callie went straight to the gourmet omelet station and designed a massive monstrosity. Zenobia selected grits, biscuits with gravy and eggs while Penny put together a fruit salad from the selection of fresh fruits.

"What is that?" Ethan reeled and laughed at the massive omelet on Callie's plate.

"Lobster, shrimp, salmon..." she named while Jovita grimaced. Callie saw the look on her face and scooped a forkful for her. "Have some?"

"No thank you!" she declined. She did notice how Ethan and Penny deliberately didn't speak and jumped to a conclusion that something happened between the two. The banter over brunch was light but once the food was eaten it was time to get down to business.

"Let's cut through to the chase," Ethan announced. That was Jovita's cue so she produced the paperwork as he spoke. "I think your decision to record independently is a good one. We will definitely be one of the bidders once the project is completed. Separate from that, I want to manage you guys."

With that Jovita handed each girl an identical management contract, save their individual names. He read from his copy to outline the industry standard twenty percent fee he would receive. It worked out to be pretty much the same as if he would have managed them all collectively as a group.

P-money and C-money both had strong solo careers ahead of them. Z-money was no less talented but didn't share the same star power as her friends. She would have a solo career of her own but it was Kelly Rowland compared to two Beyonces.

"This means we front money for incidentals along the way. We only make money if you make money," Jovita was saying but Penny was already signing her name.

"Word?" Callie asked since they hadn't even reached the second page. It was their own individual decision who to let manage them, she was just surprised she made it so quickly. Her shoulders shrugged and she finished signing. All that was left were Jovita and Ethan's signatures and she was official.

"This say twenty percent for movies?" Zenobia asked and squinted at just how big this could be. She had wanted to be on the big screen since she was a little girl.

"Yes because I'll be the one getting you a movie deal. Like Jovita said, we only make money when you do. So I want you to make as much money as possible," he explained and added. "And if it costs money to make money, I'll be the one spending it!"

Zenobia had heard enough too and plucked the pen from Penny's hand. All heads turned to Callie next.

"Continue," Callie said since there was still more to the contract. Ethan picked up where he left off.

He only made it to the next page when Callie's phone began to buzz. She only looked at it to see who would have to wait until later since she was in a meeting. She ignored the foreign number and moved to mute the phone but the same number called back immediately. Where she came from this meant something bad had happened so she needed to check.

"One sec," she said apologetically and took the call.

"Callie Wilson?" an unknown voice asked. Hearing her full name pasted a look of concern on her face that concerned her friends.

"Yeah?" she tentatively replied.

"I'm detective Morae with the Atlanta police department," she informed and nearly got hung up on.

"Yeah?" Callie asked again just as hesitantly as the last one.

"You are listed as next of kin for a Dominique Johnson..." was as far as she got before Callie dropped her phone.

"What?" Zenobia reeled and rushed to her friend's side. Penny picked up the phone to see what the what was.

"Hello?" she asked sharply. She listened intently and got the information.

"Is everything OK?" Ethan asked, ready to fix whatever he could.

"No. We have to go down to Grady hospital," Penny said and took Callie by the hand. She was still firmly clutching the contract in hand when her friends whisked her away.

"There," Penny pointed out when they entered the hospital waiting room. The forty-ish black lady looked like a cop even before Penny confirmed the badge on the chain around her neck.

"Who would shoot Dominique?" Callie wondered aloud since the last time they were here was when Lacrecia got shot.

"Hmp!" Zenobia huffed since Dominique still wasn't one of her favorite people. She and Callie may have bonded out of their up north connection but she could take her or leave her. Now that they cut off their weed supply it was a definite leave her.

"Detective Morae?" Penny asked as they approached.

"Yes?" the cop answered like a cop and made it a question. Another reason people don't like cops, besides the whole shooting down unarmed black people.

"Callie Wilson," she said and got a curious squint; she didn't look like a Wilson.

"Is she dead?" Callie just wanted to know.

"She got shot?" Zenobia added. The cop looked between the three and decided on Callie.

"Not dead, not shot. Took a pretty bad beating tho. Broken jaw, ribs," she said. "You know who would beat her like that?"

"Nah," all three said at the same time while thinking Mike's name in their minds.

"Of course not," the detective said and handed Callie her card. "If you can think of anything..."

"I won't call you," Callie finished after she walked away. She flicked the card on the floor near a few more of her cards and went to the nurses station. "Dominique Johnson?"

"Room 312," the multitasking woman said without having to look up.

Callie was a true New Yorker and knew the stairs are always quicker than an elevator unless you're going above five floors. 312 meant the third floor so she struck out up the stairwell. She bypassed the nursing station and walked into the room.

"Dayum!" Penny shrieked when she saw the woman in the bed. She looked like Martin on the episode when he boxed Tommy the Hitman Hearns. Her knots had knots and there were bruises on her bruises. The outburst caused her eyes to flicker open. Dominique saw Callie and attempted to smile. Not an easy task with a broken jaw.

"Owwee!" she moaned and blinked in gratitude.

"Mike did this to you? Because of me?" Callie growled.

"Cuz herself. You ain't got shit to do with them folks!" Zenobia cut in, followed closely by Penny.

"Not after they cut us off!" she added for a total of four cents.

"It's ok. I'll be fine," Dominique grunted through clenched teeth since her jaws were wired shut.

"Good, we'll be downstairs," Zenobia huffed and spun for the door. She really was happy the woman didn't die but they just weren't friends either. Penny offered Dominique a soft smile and left behind Zenobia.

"What happened?" Callie asked once they were alone.

"Mike wanted me to take the car back. To pressure you to sign," she explained. He kept Lil Bruh and his other artists on a yo-yo by only letting them borrow cars and rent houses. Rugs he could snatch from under them at any given moment.

"I would have given it back!" Callie shrieked.

"Naw, cuz he's still cheating you with that song. He cut you out the royalties. Probably going to be millions," she revealed.

"Wow!" she reeled. Now the lessons Ethan was just

stressing made that much more sense. Independent or not, she needed a good manager to represent her. That's when she realized she was still clutching the management contract in her hand.

"GUESS WHAT!" ZENOBIA ASKED IN WIDE EYED EXCITEMENT when Callie finally joined them in the waiting room. There was nothing more to wait for so they stood.

"She fucked Ethan," Callie shrugged. "Or at least sucked him."

"Uh, fucked! Twice," Penny proudly proclaimed. She never intended to quite wait for marriage, just hadn't been ready. Nor did she want to be conquered like some mountain, where dudes reached her peak and wrote her off. She didn't regret her decision in the least. Even if she was a bit sore.

"Wow!" Callie blinked, but she had news of her own. Once they reached the car she revealed it.

"What's this?" Zenobia asked when she presented the paperwork. Penny came over to read along with her. They immediately recognized both the document along with the obvious changes.

"The fuck?" Penny reeled at Ethan's company and logo being crossed out at the top. Diamond Management was handwritten in familiar handwriting next to it.

"I mean, y'all can read..." Callie quipped and let them read. It was the same contact, same terms, except she Substituted Dominique every place Ethan was listed. At the end were both of their signatures as well as a nurse.

"Wow!" both Penny and Zenobia exclaimed. There was

nothing more to be said, so they said nothing as they rode back over to the hotel to pick up their cars.

"Is everything OK?" Ethan asked when they finally returned. Jovita had left to handle business but he told Penny he would wait. Penny and Zenobia both turned to Callie. This was her story, so they would let her tell it.

"Yeah," Callie said hopefully as she extended the contract.

"Oh?" he immediately asked of the change of the heading. His head nodded with himself as he read through the contract for any structural changes. Finding none when he reached the signatures he managed a smirk to add to the nod. He had no idea if Dominique could fulfill her end but there was an upside. "At least you know the contract is sound!"

"You're not upset?" Callie asked after the fact since it was signed and witnessed.

"Not at all. This is fundamentally the best deal anyone will give you. As long as she can keep her end, you're good," he shrugged. Truth be told she was good anyway since he represented two thirds of the group. He still only ate when they ate so he would work just as hard.

Chapter 14

"Wow!" Zenobia exclaimed when she finally turned her phone back on after completing the first of her final exams. The beef between Lil Bruh and Young Vaughn's camps was escalating all over social media. She tuned in to the latest video posted by Lil Bruh.

'I'm moving up the charts on my way for that number one spot held by the number one bitch', he said over the picture of his song reaching the number 3 spot on the charts. Young Vaughn was clearly at number one. She immediately made a call.

"Girl I just saw it!" Callie said, shaking her head on her end of the call.

"You need to tell him to chill! Vaughn don't even want no smoke. He just tryna make music!" she fussed.

"Like he's gonna listen to me!" she shot back. She still texted back and forth with him to keep the line open but hadn't been back over to see him since the last time he peed on her.

"This shit getting out of hand!" Zenobia moaned. Rap

beef was turning deadly all over the country and she didn't want to lose her man through prison or the graveyard.

"Maybe Ethan can talk to Mike?" Callie wondered and got a head shake from the guest in the dorm room.

"He loves that shit! Thinks it's good for sales," she said.

"Who is that?" Zenobia asked when she heard a voice that didn't belong to Penny.

"See you when you get back," Callie replied and clicked off. That was one bridge to be crossed later but the other one just opened the door

"Man you see what your boyfriend just posted!" Penny announced as she came in. Her face fell when she saw someone occupying the forth bed that had been empty for so long. Then recognized her, "The fuck?"

"Told you this wasn't a good idea," Dominique said through the wires holding her mouth shut.

"It's not!" Penny shouted, then quickly calmed since this same room had been a place of refuge for them all when they were down on their luck. "She's not a student tho?"

"It's just for two weeks," Callie reminded since the semester was finally over. They were looking for apartments once Zenobia made it in. "Plus, remember what Ethan said about us still selling? Well she can handle that for us!"

"Fine. Just don't touch my stuff," Penny huffed and handed over her work phone before heading into the bathroom.

"Speaking of stuff. You know that nasty nigga gave them hoes my clothes! Jewelry, everything I had. Shit I had before I even met him!" Dominique moaned.

"And you still got Lil Bruh under contract!" Callie reminded.

"I do," she replied and managed a slight smile.

Mike had demanded she sign the artist over to him that night and she refused. He set out to beat it out of her but she didn't budge. It really would be over her dead body and almost was. She was lucky one of the young girls had enough compassion to call for an ambulance. She still took her clothes and purses though.

It was Dominique who had the experience and education in artist management. Mike just had the money and the muscle. Death was sweeter to her than walking away with nothing. If he wanted her contracts he would have to pay for them now.

"What you ain't saying...." Zenobia was asking as she stormed in but her answer was sitting on the spare bed. "Huh?"

"Our new roommate," Penny quipped as she joined them in the room. Callie explained to her as she had explained to Penny.

"Here!" Zenobia quickly agreed and handed over her work phone as well. It was buzzing as she did from the heavy demand. Runs she would gladly let someone else make.

"I need a car," Dominique informed through her clenched teeth. Her car was confiscated along with everything he gave her.

"Damn Mike," Callie said and shook her head. She needed clothes, toiletries, underclothes and now a car.

"Rent one. Business expense," Penny said since it was worth not having to run all over town serving customers.

"Thanks," Callie said, full of affection since the gesture of kindness was directed to her, not so much as Dominique.

"Please take care of Savage hoe ass! He having a weed

emergency!" Zenobia fussed and Penny cosigned since he had been blowing her up as well.

"Word," Callie agreed since he had been hitting her as well. "Z can you go get it, while I take her to get a car?"

"Yes sir baws!" Zenobia sang in her best Stepin Fetchit voice. Something she did whenever Callie got bossy.

"Want meez to shine ya shooze baws?" Penny added and cracked up.

"Naw, but you can call that trick and let him know we're sending her," she said and led Dominique out the door.

"Why y'all keep calling dude a hoe, and trick?" Dominique asked when they reached the car.

"Cuz he's gonna try you up when you get there. Be eating girls out he don't even know!" she explained.

"Say word?" Dominique grunted under the wires. Mike hadn't touched her in months since he was having his way with all the groupie love. "Shoooot!"

"I hear ya!" Callie laughed and took her over the campus car rental places. "They ain't got no Benzes or..."

"Girl, I used to drive a Escort with no power steering! Watch how I get it out of the mud!" Dominique said triumphantly and raised her chin. It was the first semblance of the boss she met back in Jersey. The weed was ready when they got back to the room and Penny decided to give her a brief tutorial on how to sell weed.

"We count the money before handing him anything. He shops a couple times a week but still," she was saying until she saw how Zenobia was looking at her. "What?"

"Girl, she was our plug! She knows what she is doing!" she laughed.

"Oh, OK. I'm finna go get laid then," she said and headed out.

"This is the building and apartment," Callie said as she handed the info over. Dominique tilted her head curiously when she recognized it.

"This is Ethan's address?" she asked even though quite sure.

"Yeah. How do you know?" Callie asked in reply.

"Mike is obsessed with him! Knows his every move," she said ominously. Callie made nothing of it so she set off to serve the weed. Callie finished making calls along her route so the customers expected the new face.

"Where are you guys? I need them five yesterday!" Savage pleaded in a panic.

"Nigga weed don't grow on trees! Well, maybe it does but still. You just got five the other day!" Callie snapped.

"And I'll probably need five more tomorrow!" he said since he was moving a good flow of weed. Davinci was his number one customer by far.

"Anyway, it's on the way. My cousin Dee is bringing it over," she explained and nearly clicked off until a wicked thought twisted her mouth into a smile. "Oh, and she just broke up with her man. Don't try to take advantage of her with that mean tongue game of yours!"

"Who me?" Savage asked as he looked around for his gray shorts.

"Dee?" Savage asked hopefully when he saw the pretty woman through the monitor.

"Yeah," she replied and the door buzzed. She pulled it open and headed down to the elevator bank. She checked the paper once again when the door opened and pressed the button for his floor. A few moments later she was walking down his hallway. The door opened and Savage posed against the door frame. He had primed up a nice semi erection to make a good first impression.

"You must be Savage!" she laughed and gripped his dick on the way in. "Where's the bread playa?"

"Huh?" Savage asked, confused from the combination of her speaking through clenched teeth and touching his dick. Plus her round ass was just as distracting.

"The money my dude," she explained and gritted a smile to show the wires and explain that part too.

"Oh yeah," he remembered and popped himself on the head. He produced the cash and watched as she expertly counted it. Once it reached what it was supposed to she pulled the bag from her shoulder and pulled out the five pounds he just paid for. It made space in the bag for the cash.

"Nice doing business with you," Dominique said once she closed the bag.

"You can chill for a sec, if you want?" Savage asked, looking her up and down. He licked his whole lips to show what he meant by chill. Then checked his watch to see if he had time to chill since a customer was coming for the weed.

"Don't bite off more than your young ass can swallow 'youngin," Dominique warned. "I'm backed up too! Shit, I'll rock your world boy!"

"Don't speak about it, be about it," he dared and she politely stepped out of her pants. She began to lay back on the sofa, then changed her mind and position. She got on her hands and knees and tooted the booty up.

Lunch was served so Savage dropped down and ravaged her lonely vagina from the back. His twirling tongue took her there in a matter of minutes. He pulled a condom from under the sofa cushion and rolled it down his stiff dick.

"Give it to me!" she urged and arched her back even further. Savage used one hand to hold a curvy hip and the other to guide him inside the soaked love glove.

"Shit!" he exclaimed when she gave him a good squeeze. Then let up so he could work it out. And work he did until the sounds of skin slapping and juice box gushing reverberated around the room.

'Finish him!' Dominique's vagina announced when his moans increased and his stroke grew choppy. She contracted her box like a vice and finished them both.

"Argh!" Savage grunted and held on like a cowboy breaking a wild horse. He pumped the condom full of toy soldiers while she writhed and shook below.

"OK bruh," Dominique advised and tapped his hip to announce the ride was over. He easily extracted himself from her box and went to remove the condom. She used his shirt to wipe the wet mess from between her legs.

"Yo, you can..." Savage was saying as he came back out but Dominique and her good pussy were gone. "Move in if you want."

He was still laughing at his little joke when the doorbell rang again. He yelled over to come in and in walked Davinci. There was an awkward moment when they both looked down at his bare dick and back up.

"Excuse that, I was just, thought you were..." he said as he picked his pants up and pulled them on. He pulled his shirt over his head and got a full face of slime from when Dominique used it to clean up.

"Yeah uh, got that?" Davinci asked at the neat pile of

pounds on the table. These five made the magic number he was looking for. He held up his end of the bargain by holding up the cash.

"That's you there homie," he said and accepted the brand new bills. He had just begun counting when there was a knock on the door.

"I'll get it. They're with me," Davinci said and made his way over to open it. Savage looked up from his count just as federal agents entered with badges out. They all had guns but knew they weren't needed for this guy.

"Michael Savage, you have the right to remain silent..." Davinci said as another agent placed him in cuffs.

"The magic number!" yet another agent announced when he verified it was five more pounds to add to all the other pounds they purchased over the last few months. "Good job Robbie!"

"Robbie?" Savage asked even more confused by the happenings happening in the living room.

"Yeah as in agent Robbie Gunter," Davinci explained and pulled his own badge. Savage sat and moped while the agents spread out and searched his unit. It wasn't the usually destructive search and seizure of most drug bust. They didn't turn over sofas or bust up TVs like they do in the hood. No drawers were dumped out, no cushions cut open and shredded.

"Guess I'm in a little trouble huh?" Savage sighed as he looked at the five pounds of weed. Then over to the most likely marked bills that would be used against him in a court of law just like anything he said. He was definitely going to have to call his rich daddy and let him pull some of those strings he had around this city.

"Little, nah," Robbie said, shaking his head. "I've

bought enough high grade marijuana from you to send you away for twenty years."

There was a brief silence to let that soak in. Savage used the time to add and multiply all the transactions they made since they met. Then how they met and he realized that his friend Olly had set him up. Traded him to get out of a simple possession charge. Robbie watched Savage's temple jump as he processed his dilemma. Once the stew was just about right he added the next ingredient.

"Or probation," he tossed out and stood to look around with his comrades. He had never ventured past the living room so he explored a little bit.

"Your friend's a real dick slinger!" an agent announced as he flipped through Savage's phone via USB cord attached to a laptop.

"Nice!" Robbie agreed with the array of vaginas in his gallery. A few more agents came over since they were guys and guys like vaginas.

"Dayum!" the men all reeled and grimaced when a bumped up box filled the screen.

"What? She said it was a hair bump?" Savage asked.

"More like herpes bump," one warned while another added, "Hope you didn't eat that!"

"He ate it!" they all exclaimed at the next video of him licking around the lumped up labia. Luckily for Dominique and a few dozen others he wasn't full-time contagious.

"Welp, time to head down to the station. Not a very long drive so you'll have to think quick," Robbie advised Savage as he helped him to his feet.

"Think about what?" he asked since there was nothing to think about as far as he knew. He was in trouble so he would call his dad to fix it.

"You're just a middleman. Selling through another middleman. We want the plug. Trade up and you'll be back home and back in business tonight. You can keep selling, keep entertaining the ladies..." Robbie started.

"Or, your soft ass will most likely get raped in jail," another finished. They had performed that spiel so many times it was flawless. "They say if you relax..."

"What I gotta do!" Savage pleaded in protection of his bung hole. That brought smiles to faces and they uncuffed him so as not to draw attention as he was taken away.

Chapter 15

"How a nigga who pee the bed think he fucking with Young Vaughn? What is you, five years old or something'

"Uh-oh!" Penny announced and tried not to laugh at the latest post in the escalating beef between the two camps.

"Awe see! Now Lil Bruh is gonna swear I put his business out!" Callie fussed. Vaughn didn't mention him by name but everyone knew who he was talking about.

"I ain't even say nothing!" Zenobia vowed. "I promise we don't have time to talk about the next nigga when I'm over there!"

"Too busy being nasty!" Penny laughed. She was one to talk since sex was like a new toy for her. She was wearing Ethan out every chance she got.

"Naw, actually he's helping me with my rhymes," she reminded. "School's out next week. It's time to hit the studio!"

"Word!" Callie cosigned since she had been working on her own flow between final exams. She still entertained Lil Bruh on the phone just so she could get his help on her rhymes. He offered to write her rhymes for her but she declined.

"Hells yeah! Ethan has been making me study different songs like it's one of my classes," Penny sighed. It seemed tedious at the moment but he was teaching her the fundamentals of making hits.

"As far as Lil Bruh, it could have been anybody who put that out! You know those groupies can't hold water!" Dominique added. She wanted to be a part of the conversation but regretted it when she saw Zenobia flinch. The painful truth was the two popular rappers did share from the same group of groupies.

Zenobia shook it off since she spent more nights there with him than here with them. Groupies were in the past since he had no time to entertain them. Now, it was Penny's turn to flinch when a beep informed her of an email.

"My dad's lawyer," she announced before opening. Dominique had no idea what was going on but the change in temperature told her it was something. "Court date. I gotta go to California."

"We gotta go to California!" Callie corrected. They had one more day of exams and the year was done.

"Which means we need to make a decision!" Zenobia reminded.

"Atlantic Station!" Callie and Penny voted. Much to Dominique's relief since it was the only four bedroom apartment they looked at. She was glad they included her and was earning her keep by running the weed sales for them. She could easily handle her forth of the four thousand dollar a month rent

"Well, while y'all study I need to get some bricks and make these runs!" Dominique announced loud enough to make her contribution to this jam.

"I'll take her," Penny said since she was going out. They didn't exactly distrust Dominique but didn't give her a key to the storage unit either. They grabbed their keys and headed on out.

"Oh lawd her come P-wanna-be-black-money!" the same light skin girl mocked when she saw Penny and Dominique on the way out.

"Get off my dick! Err time you see me you got some slick shit to say!" Penny pouted.

"White girl finna cry!" another girl laughed like she just wasn't singing along to her on the radio. Loving the song seemed to add to the hate. Haters are funny like that since most times it's just misunderstood love. Dominique took a second to ascertain what was going on but needed no time to intervene.

"Y'all leave her alone. She didn't say anything to you," she offered peacefully.

"Who you 'sposed to be, hergrandmama?" light skin reeled.

"Grand, I'm..." Dominique pouted and touched her face. She was only thirty five but to twenty year olds that's pretty much the same.

"Mind yo business auntie!" the other demanded and stepped up. Dominique looked at Penny to see how she wanted to handle it. Little did she know Penny had left the building. She was now with P-money and P-money wanted all the smoke.

"Let's just fight then!" P-money popped off and popped light skin in her pink lips. The bottom one exploded and filled her shirt with blood. The other girl budged like she wanted to jump in but Dominique jumped on her ass. The commotion was heard all over the building before spilling outside.

"That's us!" Zenobia shouted when she looked down and saw eight girls throwing punches at P-money and Dominique. She and Callie rushed down and evened the odds.

Once again cameras caught footage of the Pretty Thugs thuggin. Campus police showed up and got some footage of their own before finally breaking it up. They separated the two sides and took statements. Not that it mattered when the Deen rolled up.

"Not y'all again?" he reeled when he saw the usual suspects.

"We..." Zenobia began but Callie beat her to it.

"Whooped them hoes asses! They started, we finished!" Callie announced triumphantly and stood.

"And I told you!" he said and paused to pluck a wing from the bucket.

"Yeah, yeah. You told us," Penny said and stood as well. She walked right up to him and grabbed a wing for herself and went inside to pack.

"Guess I will have to stay at Vaughn house until the first," Zenobia sighed like it was a chore. It wasn't since she was having regular sex for the first time in her life.

"I'm sure Ethan will put up with me for a few nights?" Penny wondered. In truth it was even less since they had a flight to catch out west.

"We'll just get a room," Callie huffed since she had no intentions on getting peed on again.

Meanwhile, Misty got notification of the pending court date too. She picked out her favorite lip gloss and got to work.

"I'M HERE TO SEE MR HASKEL!" THE BUSTY BLONDE demanded as she sashayed up to the reception desk.

"Excuse me?" the receptionist asked in utter confusion. She knew who her boss was just fine but the spaghetti straps of her dress were struggling to hold the huge breast.

"They didn't say anything," she fussed. She had spent a small fortune turning her itty bitty titties into the gallon milk jugs, but they didn't talk.

"I'm sorry, I," the woman offered just as one of the straps snapped and set a titty free. "Ooh!"

"Is everything... Whoa!" the attorney was asking until he saw the big breast standing firm in front of him.

"I'm sorry!" she lied even though was remiss that her designed wardrobe malfunction, malfunctioned prematurely. Her voice finally stole the lawyer's attention from the big brown nipple that pulled his mouth open. He looked up and saw a familiar face.

"Mrs Manning?" he asked even though he recognized the face. He shook off the obvious and asked a better question. "What are you doing here?"

"Well, you represented my late husband and I have some questions?" she whined and twisted a bleached blonde lock in her finger.

"He now represents Penelope Manning in the estate..." his reception snapped, but got cut off.

"No, no, I can answer a question!" he interjected before she dismissed the woman. He used to love it when she accompanied her late husband to his office. Mr Manning would sit at his desk while she sat on the sofa behind him, crossing and uncrossing her legs. Misty cupped her bare titty and followed him inside.

"This is highly inappropriate," the woman huffed and took her lunch.

"I'm not sure what I..." Mr Haskel was saying as they entered the office. He forgot the rest of it when he saw the tiny dress fall around the six inch heels.

He blinked down at the dress while processing the implications. Not about how inappropriate it was for her to even be here since she had her own lawyer. No, if the dress was on the floor that meant she had to be naked. His eyes ran nearly a mile up the long, tanned legs before reaching a freshly shaved and extra plump vagina.

"I uh, um," he stammered.

"All those times you tried to peep under my dress and now you're at a loss for words?" she laughed. She pulled his hand and let him palm her pussy.

"Geez!" he reeled when her box seemed to suck his finger inside. He gave it a few pumps but couldn't resist himself.

"That's right!" She cheered when he devoured the mix of fluids off the finger since her latest lover bust a nut in her that morning.

"Let me eat?" he asked with his voice horse from desire.

"Shit, ok," she shrugged. It wasn't what she had planned but she wasn't turning down any head either. She made her way over to the sofa and bent over. The greedy lawyer pulled her ass cheeks apart and dove in, tongue first. He didn't specify what he wanted to eat, but clarified when he attacked her anus. Ironically it was a lot cleaner than the vagina next door. It wasn't long until a shuddering orgasm dropped her on the sofa.

"My turn!" he cheered like it was his turn to get the controller for the PlayStation. Well, not really because a blow job is better than PlayStation. A blow job and PlayStation at the same time is actually the best of both worlds. A little distracting, but that's OK.

'Gawk, gawk, gawk,' her larynx said as he stood over her on the sofa and fucked her face.

Misty was a capital H to the o, so she grabbed his hips and slammed him in and out of her own throat. Until she pressed down on her tonsils and skeeted for dear life.

"Fuck!" the lawyer grunted and grinded on her esophagus. She didn't need to swallow since he skeeted so far down her throat. So she spit the rapidly deflating dick from her mouth so she could speak.

"Now that's out the way, I need your help," she stated while tying a knot in the thin strap, to keep her escaped titty in.

"With?" he asked as he tucked his dick away and fixed his slacks.

"The estate. My lawyer says you can help us out? The bigger my cut, the bigger your cut," she explained.

"Yeah, no. I can't help you. All briefs are in. It's up to a judge now," Mr Haskel said. Inside he was chuckling at the free blow job.

"Judge huh," she sighed. Misty had blow jobs to spare so she didn't mind wasting one. "Male judge?"

"Actually, yes. Judge McNamara. Fair fellow," he nodded since he was sure he would be able to undo the damage to the estate that Misty and her lawyers had done.

"Oh OK," she said and turned to leave. She was glad it was a male judge since males have dicks. She was headed straight over to the courthouse to see if she couldn't improve her chances with him.

\

Chapter 16

"You guys be safe!" Dominique pouted when they reached the security gate at the airport. She reached out and hugged Callie tight to send her off. Penny was next but she got a stiff arm from Zenobia.

"Too soon," Zenobia told her but the light hearted laugh that came with it said she was softening up to the woman. Especially since her dough was stacking as a result of Dominique's hustle. Anytime one of those phones rang she got out and made the sale.

"First class ladies..." Penny announced as she handed out boarding passes.

"Guess when you're dating the CEO..." Callie laughed.

"Naw see! I bought the tickets myself!" Penny proudly proclaimed. Now that the estate would finally be settled she could go back to her old spending habits.

"So, you won?" Zenobia asked hopefully.

"No way I can lose. My dad would never cut me out of

his will! The judge will see right through that crap!" she declared.

"Look what my baby just texted..." Zenobia cooed and showed the picture Young Vaughn sent in his outfit for the night. He was performing at the hottest club in the city and had to look nice.

"He dope!" Callie cheered for her friend. Young Vaughn was a good dude and made her friend happy.

They spent the next few hours posting and documenting their travels for the growing number of followers. They had a video shoot for the song with Vaughn the moment they stepped back into the city. Then Callie had one with Lil Bruh the day after. Not to mention moving into the new apartment. Just a taste of the jet set world they were getting themselves into.

The hectic schedules put the girls to sleep before the jet reached cruising altitude. They slept most of the ride and watched one of Fifty Cents fifty million shows on their phones.

"Ugh!" Callie grimaced when she spotted Sarah waiting in the terminal.

"Be nice. I told her I was coming to town," Penny said as her childhood friend rushed towards her.

"Hey Penelope!" Sarah shouted and hugged her nearly off her feet.

"Sup Sarah. You remember Cal..." Penny greeted in return but got cut off.

"So nice to see you! That song has been on the radio every day!" she cheered and started singing the hook to the Young Vaughn song they were featured on.

Callie just shrugged her shoulders at the snub since it didn't matter to her. She didn't like the girl anymore than she didn't like them. Zenobia missed most of the exchange since she had been on the phone with Vaughn since the wheels touched the ground. Callie was on her own so she mocked the white girl's banter, behind their backs.

"Better not fuck nare one of them damn groupie hoes after the show!" Zenobia demanded.

"Man, why would I? You keeping a nigga straight!" he replied and took a toke from the blunt. Zenobia wasn't as freaked out as some of the groupies but she more than made up for it in cleanliness. Which was important since they had a couple bouts of unprotected sex since she was sleeping over. It's nice to be able to roll over into some pussy in the middle of the night but you have to be careful with that.

"Swear!" she insisted and stopped in her tracks. "Say I Young Bartholomew Vaughn, do solemnly swear."

"You done gave me a whole new name huh!" he laughed since Young Vaughn was actually born Vaughn Young. He could see her stopping traffic and gave her what she wanted. "On God I ain't finna fuck nare hoe, sloe, mow, snow, nothing!"

"OK then! See you in a couple days," she said and blew him a kiss. She hung up and caught up just when they reached Sarah's new ride.

"Uh, a two seater?" Penny wondered. "I told you my friends were with me!"

"I'm your friend. Those are place holders! Let them catch a bus to Watts or Compton," Sarah said as if they weren't standing here. All three waited for a punchline or giggle to indicate she was joking. None came because she wasn't.

"You finna catch these hands!" Zenobia growled and stepped up.

"Chill ma. She's not even worth it!" Callie said before she could give the girl a well deserved pop.

"Don't you mean ain't 'worf it yo!" Sarah mocked in a faux New York accent. Now it was Zenobia holding Callie back, preventing her from getting popped. Some pops can't be stopped though.

"Bitch!" Penny grunted and delivered the pop. "You were a fucking place holder! These are my friends!"

"That's why your dad married trailer trash!" Sarah shot back once she was safely inside the car.

"That's why your dad ate my ass!" Penny shouted after her as she pulled off. A mother scrambled to cover her child's ears but it was too late. Someday soon she was going to have to explain how someone ate someone else's ass. "I hope Misty is at the house!"

"I thought the lawyer said she wasn't?" Callie remembered since it was the only reason they were staying there during their brief stay.

"Hope she is so we can whoop her ass!" she explained as they marched over to the row of taxis waiting to tax people. They caught one and headed over to Brentwood.

"Here? You guys are getting ready to get your party on!" the Uber driver remarked when he pulled to a stop in front of Penney's childhood home.

"What the..." Penny gasped when she looked up from her phone.

"Fuck!" Callie and Zenobia finished for her when they pulled their eyes from their own screens.

"Man, I was at a party here one time that lasted two days!" he was saying as they piled out and pulled out their bags.

The once gated home was wide open since the gate was stuck open. It looked like it had been knocked off track by a vehicle. It could have been any one of the vehicles strewn around the driveway. Bags of garbage never made it to the curb to be taken away so they attracted flies and bees. It now looked much like the trailer park Misty grew up in.

"You know what..." Penny growled as she sat her bag down. Her friends did wonder what until she put her tennis shoes on.

"Oooh!!" they chimed and got ready for battle as well. Once they were suited and booted they stomped inside looking for a fight. They may have been prepared for battle but they were not prepared for what they saw when they stepped inside.

"Come on man!" Penny moaned when she witnessed the utter ruin. It looked like a trailer park alright, after a tornado swept through.

"The fuck is that smell?" is all Callie wanted to know.

"I'm pretty sure it's that!" Zenobia grimaced and pointed to a corner. A mix of urine, feces and vomit had festered into a new creation with a plant beginning to grow from the top.

"The party house," Penny nodded along with the Uber driver's words. They went room to room finding more damage and destruction, but no one to beat up.

"Now that's just gross!" Callie reeled and wretched when they reached the master bedroom. The huge, California king mattress looked like a Charles Manson crime scene from the remnants of period sex.

"This was my dad's favorite suit," Penny pouted when she saw the Brooks Brothers suit cut into shorts.

"Come on," Zenobia urged and pulled Penny away. Down the stairs and towards the front door while Callie summoned another car.

They got her out of there before she could see what became of her old bedroom. It had been turned into a shooting gallery for meth, heroin and anything else people wanted to inject. The house was uninhabitable so they caught the next Uber to the nearest hotel.

"The party house!" the Uber driver cheered when he picked up his guest. He got no reply and kept on talking. "When is the next shindig?"

"Shut the fuck up!" Callie snapped. Zenobia followed up with, "Before we shindig in your ass!"

No one wants a shindig in their ass, so he promptly shut the fuck up and drove them to their destination.

"It's on tonight!" Vaughn announced excitedly as he checked his drip in the mirror.

"It's up if these fuck niggas say anything!" Cool growled. He was a shooter, not a rapper and had no tolerance for the war of words waging on the internet.

Lil Bruh had moved up to threats, and taking pictures with guns. Cool never took a picture with a gun in his whole life, but had got his off on more than one occasion. He wasn't actually a body guard since he and Young Vaughn had been friends since they were young. Then again, who better to guard your body than someone who genuinely loves you.

"Man, fuck them folks!" Vaughn laughed. He had the number one on the radio and a show in the hottest club in the city.

"Mmhm," Cool nodded. He still wanted to bust something but would settle for some after the after party sex. Vaughn may have settled down with Zenobia but he was free, single and ready to mingle.

"Gonna get a bulletproof whip like Young Dolph had," Vaughn was saying as they headed out to his car. The thought of it not saving him from getting shot hit them both as they got in. Vaughn may have been a rising star but still liked to drive his own whip.

Cool rode shotgun literally since he had a shotgun laid across his lap. A forty caliber tucked into the small of his back and a highly illegal, fully automatic submachine gun in the trunk. If it's whatever with me'was a person, it would be him.

The club was so packed the people at the end of the block long line had no chance of getting in. Their party would be right there on the sidewalk since outside speakers allowed them to hear the music. A cloud of weed smoke hovered above like Seattle fog, while people took sips of their BYOB. One industrious hustler went up and down the long line selling cold beer and rolled joints.

"VIP shit," Cool laughed as Vaughn bypassed the bullshit and pulled around to the back of the club. He parked next to the owner's car but Cool popped out before he could come to a complete stop. He looked around for danger and announced, "Clear!"

"This nigga think he secret service!" Vaughn laughed and got out. Went in and jumped straight on stage.

Cool kept an eye out for opps while Young Vaughn wrecked shop. He whipped the crowd into a frenzy as he ran through some of his new material. The show closed with his radio hit with the Pretty Thugs. The audience moaned when they saw the girls weren't there but took up the slack and sang the hook for them.

"Wonderful!" Ethan clapped when he joined him and Jovita in the VIP section. He slid into the booth while Cool kept an eye out for Lil Bruh and company. They weren't performing and weren't fans so their presence would be considered an act of aggression. He was ready to get aggressive himself.

"Thanks fam!" he said and shook his hand. Then accepted the flute of champagne Jovita extended. "Video still on?"

"Yes sir!" Ethan happily nodded and took a swig of his own glass of bubbles. They basked in the growing limelight and watched the people party.

"Heeeeey Young Vaughn," a pretty groupie sang and popped her thick lips as she reached the table. A heavy coating of gloss reminded him of a tire with fresh armor all shine. Cool hovered closely in case she was a threat. Despite the fact that her tiny dress couldn't conceal her nipples so no way she had a weapon.

"Sup shawty," he greeted and waited for her request. One thing he was quickly learning about stardom was that someone always wanted something from him. Aunts, uncles and cousins all needed money, cars or rent paid. He knew this groupie wanted an autograph, picture or free shirt. He was wrong though because she was here to give.

"I'm tryna come with you!" she said plainly. There was a literal line of ladies wanting the same thing but she made it first.

"I got a girl," he shot back quickly. Zenobia was with her girls in California but she took his heart with her. He was quite proud of his personal growth as he turned his back on some free pussy.

Ethan cracked a smirk at the answer. He saw how much more focussed he had been since he no longer had the distraction of various vaginas to tend to. Something he could relate too since he was digging Penny's company.

"Let me just suck your dick baby. Please!" she pleaded in his ear and clasped her hands together like it was a prayer.

"Do what!" Vaughn barked to punk her out. Sometimes some people hear how they sound when they say some shit and won't say that shit again. She obviously wasn't some people though.

"Just let me suck your dick. I respect your relationship but, just for a few minutes baby! I love your music! I wanna get you in my mouth!" she moaned and popped those thick lips again.

"I'm finna sign an autograph on her uh," Vaughn was saying as he stood.

"Tonsils," Jovita assisted since she was an assistant boss.

"I'm coming with you," Cool announced gruffly.

"Naw, I'm coming alone shawty," the rapper laughed. His partner didn't though and passed him the forty caliber.

"Only shooting you finna do is in my mouth," the groupie purred as he led her back to the back door they entered in. He saw no need to treat the groupie like a lady so he hit the fob to unlock the locks and let her open her own door.

They met in the middle of the car where he tucked the gun in between the seat and whipped out the dick. She marveled at it for a moment then spent another moment fondling it. That wasn't the deal so he leaned back and pulled her head down.

"OK then!" Vaughn cheered when the hot mouth engulfed him. She obviously meant 'suck' in the literal sense since she applied the suction. There was nothing to do now except enjoy the favor. His eyes closed and he focused on the finish line.

The suction increased when her phone buzzed. The coincidence caused his eyes to open just as two men crept towards the car. He blinked to reset the vision since sometimes some good head can make a man see things that aren't there. Like relationships or dudes with guns creeping up.

"The fuck!" Vaughn shouted and reached for the gun. He got a grip on the handle but the groupie grabbed it with both hands and pushed down with her full weight. Then bit down on his dick to hold him in place.

The first of many rounds sped through the windshield, straight at his face. He managed to duck out the line of fire a split second before bullets shredded his headrest. It didn't take a criminal justice degree to figure the girl was in on the hit. He fought fire with fire and bit her ear until his teeth met.

"Owe nigga!" would be her last words since she released her bite and sat up directly into the line of fire. A slug tore through her face and lodged in her brain. She fell back into his lap but her dick sucking days were over.

One shooter came over to the driver's door and snatched it open. He was met by a brilliant flash but never heard the gunshot that accompanied it. It knocked his life out the hole in the back of his head. Cool rushed out just as the second gunman made a dash for the waiting car.

"Pop the trunk shawty!" he yelled as he jumped from the rear steps. His ankle twisted badly but it would have to wait. Vaughn popped the trunk and Cool scooped the souped up gun from the trunk.

The people stuck in the long line got a front row seat to the real life action flick. Cool couldn't catch the getaway car but the bullets could. He lifted the gun and sprayed it at the rear window. The back glass splashed like water when the bullets tore through on their way to meet the passengers. The car began to slow since the driver wasn't able to drive with a bullet in his head. It careened into the parked cars and grinded to a stop.

The show was over.

Chapter 17

"*G*irl!" Penny shrieked as she ran through the hotel room.

"I know!" Zenobia said since she heard the news on her phone too. She kept calling Vaughn but his phone was going straight to voicemail since he was in the police station.

Different detectives had him repeat his story several times, looking and listening for inconsistencies so they could charge him with murder. He normally invoked his Miranda rights but Ethan told him to talk since he was in the right. He didn't need his cash cow in jail while they investigated. He and Cool cooperated completely and even turned the guns over to the cops.

"Your car pulling up!" Callie announced when she joined them. She had already summoned an Uber to take her back to the airport. She would stay to support Penny but Zenobia needed to go see about her man.

"Thanks!" Zenobia said as she scrambled to pack. She was so confused she packed all of her shoes in the bag as well.

All she heard was a deadly shooting involving rapper Young Vaughn. The disjointed social media post from witnesses who witnessed things a lot different than they transpired.

"I got this," Callie said while Penny booked the first thing smoking back east.

"It's going to be fine!" Penny assured her and snatched the trembling girl into her arms. Callie made it a group hug until the car announced it's presence downstairs.

"It will be fine!" Zenobia repeated all the way to the airport. She was halfway back across the country when she finally heard from Vaughn. He was too exhausted to fill her in now but vowed to meet her at the airport.

"I'm not going to be any good," Penny pouted when the sun began to rise on the new day. First there was the disaster at her house, the drama in Atlanta, now she had to go to court on zero sleep.

"It'll be fine," Callie offered just like she had told Zenobia. She didn't know how, but it was all she had.

"Yeah. My dad worked hard for his stuff. No way he leaves it to some trailer trash, dirty butt!" she declared. On cue Mr Haskel called from the lobby to take her to court.

"Let's ride!" Callie cheered triumphantly. The family lawyer didn't know Penny brought company but found out when they arrived in the lobby.

"Hello Penelope," Mr Haskel greeted half-heartedly and offered a lackluster hug. He and Callie connected eyes when he embraced her and she saw the deceit in his irises.

"This is my friend Callie. Callie, Mr Haskel. The family lawyer who saved my dad's estate!" Penny introduced.

"Hello Miss Callie. Nice to meet you," Mr Haskel greeted but his eyes were still lying.

"Yeah, hey," Callie dared and furrowed her brow. He folded under the stare and turned to lead them to the car.

"So, how's it looking?" Penny asked once they were under way.

"Uh oh, it, yeah, we," was all Callie heard through the stammers and stutters. She was no legal eagle but expected the worst. An hour later they got it.

'BLAH, BLAH, BLAH. SOMETHING, SOMETHING, SOMETHING...' the lawyers said as they went back and forth. Penny and Callie didn't understand most of what they heard but did notice the judge seemed more receptive to whatever Misty's lawyer's were saying.

"This bitch is asleep!" Callie thought to herself when she noticed the woman had nodded off again. She hadn't much sleep either since methamphetamines tend to keep one wide awake.

"OK, OK. I'll take a few minutes to deliberate," the judge said and stood. The bailiff was supposed to announce 'all rise' but the man moved too fast. He retired to his chambers to mull over the facts.

"Excuse me. I have to pee," Misty said and stood herself. She held her chin high enough to overlook Penny as she passed by and out of the courtroom. Callie saw the quick nod at Mr Haskel on her way out. Haskel nodded at her lawyer and turned to Penny.

Misty hit the hallway and looked both ways as if about to cross the street. She wasn't though but the coast was clear so she slipped into the judges office from the hall entrance.

She didn't knock on his chambers before opening the door but then again she was expected.

"Hey there young lady!" the judge greeted happily. He already had his dick out so she swooped down like an eagle scooping a trout from a river. Except it was a dick.

"Mmhm, mm-mm, mmhm," she hummed while she worked. The woman was nearly thirty and blow jobs were still the only work she ever held. She had sucked plenty of free dicks in her life but this one was worth millions.

"All rise!" the judge cheered when he exploded on her tonsils once again. This blow job was just one of many to have him rule in her favor.

"Mmhm!" she repeated once more and swallowed all evidence of the bribe. She stepped back into the hallway and arrived back in the courtroom just before the judge.

"All rise!" the bailiff announced like he was supposed to. All rose except Callie who held the court in contempt instead of the other way around.

"I rule in favor of the plaintiff and honor the last will and testament. The estate is hereby awarded to Mrs Misty Manning," he said and banged his gavel.

Penny sat there in stunned silence, trying to process what the words meant. Mr Haskel was speaking but she couldn't hear any of the words coming out of his mouth. He looked over at Callie for help when Penny was unresponsive.

"You some bull shit!" Callie said and made him turn red. He snatched up his papers and stormed out. His work was done and he would collect a nice piece of the pie they just split.

"Huh?" Penny asked when she looked up. She was

confused at how Mr Haskel turned into Callie but couldn't hear her words either.

"I said, we out this bitch!" she shouted and pulled her friend from the chair. "Ethan got lawyers too! We finna get to the bottom of this shit!"

"You said finna!" Penny laughed as she stood.

"Uh oh!" Callie laughed since she knew that laugh. Penny had left the building and P-money was in the house.

Callie wasn't sure what Penny was doing but obviously it needed to be done. Their first stop was a car rental for a car for the day. Not even a full day since their flight left in a few hours. Second stop was the hardware store where P-money loaded a cart up with several of the same item.

"Word?" Callie asked when she saw the full cart. She was down for whatever and shrugged. "OK Left Eye."

The third stop was a gas station to fill the five gallon gas tanks. Next stop was the house. Callie may have been down for whatever but this was Penny's beef to cook.

"Stay here," she ordered when she pulled back into the rundown mansion.

It took some doing to tote the gas cans into the house one by one. By the third trip Penny was sweating and smelled like gasoline. She had begun pouring the gas upstairs and saturated her dad's old bedroom. She worked her way down and around until the gas cans were all empty. Actually it was far more gas than necessary but some lessons come harder, or hotter than others.

"Oh lawd!" Callie laughed and shook her head when P-money emerged wearing a satisfied smirk. She was quite dramatic when she retrieved a book of matches from her pocket. She lit one and used it to light the whole book. A smile spread on her face when she tossed it back over her shoulder.

WHOOSH the fireball roared as it blew out the windows and doors. Oh, and Penny.

"Penny!" Callie cried real tears when she lost sight of her friend in the fireball. Only for a second until she came sailing through the air. Penny landed right on her head and gave herself a nice gash.

"You drive!" Penny exclaimed as she hopped up and made sure she wasn't on fire herself.

"This bitch is fucking crazy!" Callie laughed as she slid over in the driver's side. Penny dove into the back seat and she pulled away.

"Too much gas!" Penny announced, smelling like smoke. "Too much gas!"

"Mmmm," Young Vaughn moaned when he awoke to find his morning wood pressed firmly against Zenobia's firm ass. She arrived just a few hours ago and crawled right into bed.

"Mmhm, you got some explaining to do!" she said but still grinded her ass on his dick. He didn't want to talk when she got in so she respected it. After all, he did kill a man last night.

"In a sec," he said and reached down between her legs. Her vagina spoke for both of them and got wet and juicy in an instant.

"Un-uh," she hummed and twisted her lips but she was fronting because her leg lifted so he could slide in from the side like he did most mornings when she stayed over. Which was most nights except the occasional spend the night in the hotel to prove she didn't live there. The hum was chased out the room by a 'ssss' when he slid up in her.

"Shit!" Vaughn grunted once he was deep inside. That's guy talk for, 'damn you got some good pussy'. Soon mutual moans and skin slapping filled the room. It had been a rough night indeed but the soft and warm vagina made it all better. "Shit!"

"Don't, ssss, come in me!" she moaned. Just in the nic of time too because he snatched out and skeeted on the sheets. They moaned and groaned, grinded and groped for a few minutes before she spoke up again. "Now, tell me what happened!"

Bits and pieces of the events had made their way through social media. But she knew those apps distort truth like a prism does light. The number had increased from four dead to nearly ten. Someone reported Tupac was shooting a gun as well.

"Shit was crazy shawty. The chick was in on the lick. She tried to stop me from pulling my strap when them niggas rolled up," Vaughn began. He skipped the part about his dick being on her tonsils but that's to be expected. He didn't see what happened on the street since he was in shock from the dead girl in his car and the dead man lying beside it. "I killed someone!"

"Mmhm, but how did the chick get in your car?" Zenobia rewinded. She heard the whole story but focused on the girl in his car.

"Huh? Who?" Vaughn asked to stall.

"You know what. Take me home!" she fussed.

"What happened? And Ion even have my car!" he

reminded. She remembered and summoned another Uber to leave the same way she arrived.

"You swore! Solemnly swore not to fuck no bitches while I was gone!" she pouted as she dressed.

"I didn't! For real, for real! On God I didn't!" he vowed again but she was too far gone at the moment. She finished dressing and stomped towards the door. "What about the video shoot?"

"Fuck that video shoot!" she shouted but once again she was fronting. "What time! We need to shop!"

"Three. Here..." Vaughn said and scrambled for his pants. He started to peel her off something from the stacks but handed the whole thing over. It was the whole seven thousand he received for the show but he had another show tomorrow night that would make it right back.

"Mmhm," Zenobia hummed again but again, she was fronting. If he was paying her seven racks to fuck other broads he could fuck until his hearts content.

Chapter 18

"What the heck happened to you?" Zenobia reeled when she saw the bandage on Penny's forehead when they arrived from their flight.

"Long story," she said while Callie just shook her head and laughed. If she lived to be a hundred she would always remember the girl flying through the air in a fireball.

"You guys good?" Dominique asked since she begged to tag along. Zenobia wasn't ready to give in yet but they did have a good conversation about men on the way over. The older woman shared her triumphs and tragedies on the way to the airport. Zenobia picked some dos and don'ts from her life to keep for her own.

"Hell naw, but we will be!" Penny proclaimed. She had filled Ethan in already and he was already at work with his lawyers. Zenobia could tell she needed a hug and gave her one.

"Bruh, why do you smell like, fire?" she asked when she squeezed Penny tightly.

"We need a shower," Penny replied.

"Don't forget about the video shoot today!" Dominique reminded.

"I need something to wear!" Callie cheered. They headed back to the hotel to shower, change and shop.

"Look at this shit shawty!" Cool announced and shoved his phone towards Young Vaughn's face. He was on Lil Bruh's IG account where he was mourning his dead homies. The same homies that died the night before.

"Shit, I 'coulda told you that. I ain't in no beef with no one but him," Vaughn grimaced. They flicked through his pictures and saw the rapper and the same shooters who tried to kill him. Men he never had words with before in this life, yet violently sent them to the next life. It didn't sit well with Vaughn but Cool had other plans.

"That nigga gotta go!" Cool voiced. Vaughn contemplated for a moment before his shoulders shrugged. He didn't give the order but wasn't going to stop it either. He would never be able to live until this nemesis was dead.

"We need to hit this mall. Do some shopping for the video," Vaughn said and stood to leave.

"The mall though?" Cool laughed since it had been a while since they shopped in the mall. Even upscale malls like the one he had in mind. Only because Zenobia posted from the mall. She was still mad at him but tagged him anyway.

"The mall," he laughed along with him and donned something that can't be purchased in most malls.

"That white boy is serious about his bread!" Cool laughed at the bulletproof vest Ethan had sent over.

"Hell naw, we got mils to make!" Young Vaughn said and led the way out of the house. He caught a funny sensation as they stepped out. A vibration coming from every direction. Vaughn opened his mouth to express it, but didn't get a chance to say anything when cars whipped up from every direction.

"Get down!" Cool shouted since they were too exposed to make it back into the house. Vaughn went down as Cool's gun came up.

"Federal agents! Drop the gun! Arrest warrant!" the men shouted from every angle to accompany the red laser sights dancing on Cool's face and chest.

"That's the feds shawty! Chill!" Vaughn urged from his prone position.

"It's a trap shawty!" Cool insisted as he moved the gun back and forth over the several cars and even more agents. His mind registered the white faces but the recent attack on them had him shook.

"Drop the gun! Now!" an agent screamed as Cool turned with the gun. He didn't want to shoot the young man but didn't want to get shot by the young man even more. Cool continued turning the gun in his direction until he had no choice.

'Brrrr' the agent's gun ripped, sending three consecutive rounds exactly where the red laser pointed. He dropped right in front of Vaughn. Both men locked eyes but only Young Vaughn could see anything.

"Naw shawty!" Vaughn moaned as he looked into the lifeless eyes. He didn't even notice the agents on his back, cuffing his hands. He was going to be late to the mall.

※

"WHO YOU LOOKING FOR!" CALLIE DEMANDED WHEN SHE saw Zenobia bounce her head in every direction for a fourth time.

"Young Vaughn," Penny answered for her and showed Callie her post that tagged Young Vaughn with her whereabouts.

"Thought you were mad at him?" Callie wondered since she had just stormed in a few hours ago raging about how mad at him she was.

"So. Still wanna see him," she pouted. Then switched the subject to something else as they stepped into their favorite boutique.

"You need to grab something. Can't have my manager looking frumpy," Callie told Dominique.

"Yeah, you right," she agreed and selected a mid thigh skirt that showed thirty five wasn't that far from twenty five. She reached into her purse to pay for it but Callie grabbed her hand.

"This is on us," Zenobia announced since they had come up with the plan.

"I can't," Dominique declined and shook her head. She had spent twelve years with a man who gave her everything, only to take it all away.

"Ain't got no choice!" Penny quipped and placed her money on the counter.

"Gotta get your own shoes tho ma!" Callie said and headed over to the sports store in search of pink Timberlands to match their matching outfits. Penny found a pair of stilettos, while Zenobia copped a pair of throwback Fila tennis shoes. Shopping worked up an appetite so they traipsed over to the food court.

"Hey!" a girl shouted and ran towards the girls with

other girls in tow. Dominique instinctively stepped out front in case it was beef.

"Sup yo!" Callie demanded hotly while Penny morphed to P-money.

"Are y'all the Pretty Thugs!" the lead girl huffed, out of breath from the sprint.

"Ye..." Callie tried to respond but the teens lost their minds.

"Told you!" the first shouted and danced triumphantly. She lost her spot because the others rushed forward. "Can I have your autograph! Can we take a picture! Oh my God!"

This was the moment the crew understood they were on their way to stardom. They were only featured on two songs and were mobbed in the mall. The commotion caused more gawkers and onlookers. People posted, and tagged and the Pretty Thugs gained more followers on their social media accounts. It took an hour to satisfy the fans before they could get over to the food court.

"Bruh, I just got a thousand new followers!" Penny announced as the others went to check theirs.

"I need to make a page for the group," Dominique announced. She was on her job and got good footage of the autograph session.

"Thousand too!" Callie announced when she checked hers. All eyes turned to Zenobia who looked like she was in shock. "Girl what!"

"V,v,vaughn..." she stuttered since she had checked his page before checking her own.

"Let me see this!" Penny demanded and pulled her phone away. The white girl kept a nice tan but still went white when she read, "Deadly shooting at rapper Young Vaughn's house..."

✳

"NOSEY ASS NIGGAS!" CALLIE FUMED WHEN THEY PULLED UP to the circus in front of Young Vaughn's house. There were several official vehicles parked haphazardly while throngs of looky-loos lined the police tape to steal a glance. All Zenobia saw was the body bag being loaded on the gurney.

"Z!" Penny screamed when Zenobia tore off from the car. She hurdled the yellow tape like a track star then turned into a running back when she stiff armed a local cop who tried to stop her. She had made it all the way to the body bag and went for the zipper.

"Vaughn!" Zenobia wailed as she and the coroner van driver struggled over the zipper.

"Z," Vaughn called out and only made her more frantic.

"I'm here baby!" she screamed and fought even harder to open the bag since her beloved was calling her from beyond the grave.

"No baby. Up here," Vaughn announced from the front porch. Zenobia looked up, back down at the bag, then back to the man she was fighting.

"My bad," she shrugged and leapt up onto the porch to hug her man. "Oh baby! What happened..."

"Long story," he sighed as one of the agents announced the 'all clear' on the search.

Cool's body was taken away and the officials began to dissipate. The onlookers still looked on as the rest of the crew joined Zenobia and Young Vaughn inside. All eyes were on him so he began.

"They ain't 'stutting dude I 'kilt. They came to lock bruh up for the bodies he dropped and the gun," he explained as it had been explained to him. Once security footage came back from the back of the club it was clear Vaughn fired in self defense.

The security footage of what happened out on the street told a different story. It was clear that the men in the car were fleeing which meant they weren't a threat. Chasing them down equalled murder. Using the modified, fully automatic weapon made it federal.

"What the hell!" Ethan demanded as he stormed into the house. Jovita was right behind him and quickly took count of their assets.

"Sup bruh," Vaughn sighed and told the story all over again.

"Sheesh!" the boss groaned at yet another close call. "I'm canceling the video shoot until I can get you around the clock security!"

"I got 'round the clock security!" Vaughn announced and held up another gun. It was legal and licensed so the feds left it. They got what they came for even if Cool left in a body bag.

"We're going to lose the venue," Jovita recalled, since they had secured a club for the video shoot.

"Bruh, I'm good. Niggas get shot err day," Vaughn said and stood. "We got a video to shoot!"

Chapter 19

"**Y**ou got to be the lamest, softest, sucka ass nigga to ever come out the Bricks!" Mike berated on the phone. It was bad enough Vaughn botched the hit but now he was on social media moaning and mourning.

"Nah, see, they..." he scrambled for excuses. He wasn't smart enough to realize Mike put the ideas in his head and he was pushing his buttons again.

"All y'all niggas can't kill one nigga? Y'all soft as fuck! Ion know if I need no soft ass rappers on my label," he said and hung up. Mike grabbed his remote and pushed a button just like he had done in the rapper's weak mind.

"My mom's a hoe if I let this go!" Lil Bruh fumed as he paced his living room with a gun in hand. His mom actually was a hoe since she was just one of the many women from many hoods, who chose crack over their family. She roamed the streets of Newark in search of tricks and dicks to feed her bottomless pit of addiction.

"Chill Bruh," one of his remaining crew urged and ducked as he swung the gun in his hand.

"Chill my dick nigga! Boone dead! Spot dead! Black dead!" the rapper shot back and named the men laid out in the same morgue as Cool. The men he sent to do his dirty work. That's the part that ate at him the most.

"And Lovey!" one of the groupies reminded since her friend died in the car with Vaughn.

"Chill Bruh," another of his crew advised, since it had already gone too far. People were dead and there is no coming back from the dead.

"I'ma chill. Chill, OK. I'ma chill!" Bruh said and kept pacing.

"Look! They shooting a video now!" another groupie exclaimed since she followed P-money on all of her accounts. "They at the Inferno!"

"Inferno huh?" Bruh nodded and looked down at the gun in his hand. He knocked away a tear for his dead homies and headed for the door. "It's about to get hot up in that piece!"

"Bruh! Lil Bruh! Chill!" hiscrew called after him as he tore out of the house. There would be no chill tonight because he was too far gone. Literally and physically since they were talking while he was driving. All they could do was jump in the other cars and try to catch him.

"THAT WAS FIYAH SHAWTY!" VAUGHN CHEERED AT THE WRAP of another scene. The Pretty Thugs may have just sang on the hook on the song but they were the stars of the video.

That was Ethan's doing since he didn't eat unless they ate. Featuring them heavily in the video fixed a nice big plate for them to eat off.

"Mmhm," Zenobia hummed, huffed and crossed her arms over her chest. Body language for 'I don't fuck with you'.

"Come on shawty! Let that shit go! If I was in the car you know I ain't fuck the bitch!" he reasoned.

"Sure ain't fuck me in a car yet!" she puffed since she was done huffing. She was done beefing about it too since she missed him.

"I will..." he suggested as he leaned in to plant a kiss and palm her ass. "We got time 'fo this last scene?"

"Make me damn sick," Zenobia said and took his outstretched hand. She followed behind just as one of the guards Ethan hired fell instep as well.

"We got this shawty!" he told the armed man and kept on to his rental since his own car was still a crime scene.

"There go that fuck nigga right there," Lil Bruh growled when he spotted his prey. He had given up on getting past the security with his gun but here came Young Vaughn all by himself. He was so focussed on him, she didn't even register. That's why they call it collateral damage.

"Hop on in there..." Vaughn said as he held open the back door so she could enter and he could grip her ass as she did.

"Mmhm I..." Zenobia was saying before her eyes went wide with fright. Young Vaughn's mind went to his gun under his seat when he saw the fear in her eyes. It was too far, and too late when another quiet night erupted in deadly gun fire...

. . .

SA'ID SALAAM

The End

Meanwhile in Atlanta...

"Sup sweet thang," a man slurred as he approached the hottie in a drunken swagger.

"You!" the prospective pussy purred. She was ready to dismiss him until she ran the numbers. The thick chain around his neck was solid, 24k so she gave it ten racks. Two carat diamond studs in each lobe was at least another five.

The wedding band wasn't a turnoff at all since it was crusted in another couple carrots. Her head nodded when the hands of the Rolex glided around the face as it should. She moved down to the thousand dollar shirt, five hundred dollar shoes and fifteen hundred dollar boots. In her line of work she had to stay up on the latest fashion and jewels. She could determine a man's net worth in the time it took to look him from head to toe.

"Let me keep it a 'huned, I'm tryna spend a thousand," he said and swayed on his feet.

"I look like I sell pussy!" she barked back and placed her hands on her hips. Now it was his turn for a once over. The deep plunge of her neckline gave up all the titty on down to her navel. The dress barely covered all that luscious brown ass she was toting through the club.

"Yes," he nodded with his own assessment. "Mmhm, sure do!"

"It cost more than a grand tho!" she came clean and had to steady him when he swooned from the liquor in his glass. He was so drunk he probably wouldn't last long enough to get undressed. She of course would help him get undressed and make off with everything but his drawers. "For you tho..."

"I live not too far," he said and pointed, shook his head and pointed in the other direction.

"Even better!" she cheered. She had a trick for this trick if he actually took her home. She would first rob him blind. Literally everything in his house, his suits, shoes, watch, even designer glasses. Then, run to a 24 hour Walmart and copy his key. Give him a few weeks to bounce back and rob his ass again.

"Let's ride then!" he cheered happily and headed for the door.

"Un-uh, this way papi," she laughed and spun him around since he was headed for the restrooms.

"Thanks umm..." he said and hummed to help remember her name. It wouldn't help since they missed that part. "Ok I'm uh Jim. And you said um..."

"Alizae," she said as she led him to slaughter. Alizae usually used false names when she rolled drunks from the club. This guy was so wasted he wouldn't remember it by the time they reached the sidewalk. He smelled like he had a whole bottle of liquor poured on him.

"You got him?" the valet asked when Jim handed him his ticket.

"Oh, I got him a'ight!" she nodded when the ticket led to the unmistakable Bentley key fob. Alizae was now plotting on how she could get the car to New York and have it stripped before he awoke. She made a few underworld connections down in Atlanta but didn't have a chop shop just yet.

The attendant helped Jim into the passenger seat as Alizae hopped behind the wheel. Jim leaned back and began to snore as she pulled away from the club. Luckily the GPS knew the way to his home. They arrived at a two million dollar bungalow near the Atlanta zoo.

"We're home!" Alizae announced and shook him in the passenger seat. If not for the alarm monitoring signs she would have let him sleep and cleaned him out. He didn't budge so she leaned up and slapped a spark out of him.

"Mama?" he asked and looked around for Etta Mae.

"Naw, it's mami. Now let's go inside so I can put this pussy in your mouth," she said.

"K," he agreed and fell out of the passenger seat. She helped him up and over to the front door. As suspected the alarm began to beep when they opened the door. He had thirty seconds to enter the code before the whole neighborhood was peeking through their blinds. Ten seconds later the cops would be knocking at the front door.

"What's the code?" Alizae asked. She committed it to memory for next time as she entered it into the keypad. The beeping stopped and it was time for the games to begin.

"Come on in here," Jim slurred and led her into his bedroom.

"Come out them clothes papi so I can put this pussy on you!" Alizae moaned and came out of her dress with one stroke. She posed with her hands on her hips, wearing nothing but a smile and heels.

"Your snake ass is fine tho. I'll give you that," Jim offered, minus the slurred speech.

"Huh?" Alizae asked when he suddenly became sober. She had set up enough people to instantly recognize being set up herself. Her animal nature kicked in and she immediately went into flight or fight mode. This was almost expected since she had robbed so many people since coming to Atlanta. Or it could be from New York, either way it was on. She kicked off her heels and turned to run back out the same door, but that's where the man with the gun was standing.

"Oh no you don't," he said, shaking his head and lifting the gun.

"What's this about?" Alizae demanded as she tried to place the faces. She strained her memory banks but couldn't recall robbing either of them.

"Grimy ass did so much dirt, you don't even know what you are about to get killed for huh?" the man with the gun asked while Jim pulled out his phone to explain further. He found the picture and turned the phone to face her. "Remember him?"

"Never saw him before in life! Y'all got the wrong bitch!" Alizae snapped when she saw Ice on the screen.

"That's funny since you claim he raped you?" Jim asked.

"Oooooh bruh!" she played it off and waited to see where this was going.

"We can do this one of two ways," Jim said and paused for effect. This had been rehearsed already so the man with the gun jumped in.

"First, is I kill your ass! No victim, no crime!" he growled and pressed the gun against her cheek.

"Or, two?" she asked and turned her eyes back to Jim.

"Or recant your story. Ice will be the next Lebron when he hits the league! You're rape charge is fucking with hundreds of millions of dollars!" Jim shouted. "Plus I fucked up my suit pouring liquor all over myself!"

"Damn! Hundreds of millions? All I got was ten bands," she said and shook her head. The men looked confused at the revelation when she made her choice. "I'll take option two please. But, I'ma need you to throw in some bread too."

"Who paid you ten thousand to set him up?" the man with the gun wanted to know.

"What's in it for me!" Alizae dared and stuck her chest out.

"Your life," Jim replied plainly. "Because whoever did, is dead!"

Pretty Thugs 4 is up next!

DAWGS

A Novel
by
Sa'id Salaam

Dedication

Dedicated to Tisha Andrews.
Too often we dedicate to the dead and overlook the living. I want to
acknowledge one of my closest friends for your friendship. Thank you.

Seven high tech electric bikes caused all heads to turn as they whipped through the Manhattan streets. The riders all wore colorful, leather riding suits that matched their bikes and helmets. A turbine whine replaced the usually obnoxious roar of motorcycles but still added some cool to the hot and muggy summer night.

The riders scanned the lines of pretty people in front of the many nightclubs catering to the many fetishes of the city that never slept. Slick hair and gold chains lined a mainly Italian club while droves of multi shaded people waited to enter the hip hop club.

Anyone of them would have sufficed but they were headed to the Meet Market. A semi underground club that catered to their kind. Most people would drive or walk right past the venue without knowing it was even there. Those in the know just followed their nose to the hottest spot in the city. In any city since they were popping up everywhere.

The leader of the pack rode slightly ahead while the others rode two abreast behind him. He lifted the blacked out visor of the helmet and inhaled all the aromas that made up New York city. Curry mixed with arroz con pollo, baklava, gunpowder and good weed. Through it all he smelled his favorite meal loud and clear. A glance up to the sky showed a full moon in all its glory.

The lead rider pulled in front of their destination and backed his bike against the curb. He was indeed the leader so his followers followed suit and parked. They removed their helmets, putting their rugged good looks on display.

Rajeem stood a solid six foot one and had the build of an action figure. His complexion fell right in the middle of the race spectrum despite his classic African features. The high cheek bones of eastern Africa accentuated the thick lips of at least part of his ancestry. Bright, almost yellow skin gave a hint to the other part. His wavy hair had a brownish hue and flowed into a tapered beard.

"Smell that?" his sidekick Dog asked as he kicked his kickstand. He pulled his helmet off and sniffed the air.

"Yeah," Rajeem said quickly. He had actually felt it, before he smelled it. The mood of the pack darkened when a Benz with darkened windows pulled to a stop across the street. No one needed x-ray vision to see since they could smell their foes before they opened the door.

"Let's eat these clowns!" Beans asked as he unzipped his leather. He was the hothead of the pack of hotheads but Rajeem showed some restraint, for once since he was always down to ride on his enemies. Maintaining the alpha male spot took frequent acts of extreme violence.

"Some other time," he said and snarled at the men as they approached. Tonight was about satisfying another appetite so it could wait. He joined his pack in glaring at their enemies.

"Not enough, you need more people," one of the men from the Benz bragged. Lycans could be arrogant like that since they were slightly higher on the food chain.

"Some other time," Rajeem repeated and turned to enter the club with his pack on his heels.

The club may not have had a sign out front but was still filled to the gills inside. The mixed race, income and species club catered to the discreet of different breeds. This was one of the few places on the planet where they all coexisted.

The leader led the way up to the VIP section reserved for alpha males like himself. A lessor pack abandoned a table when they saw him approaching. The easy way always beats the hard way so they took it.

"Drinks on me!" Rajeem announced and tossed a stack of hundreds in the air. It was similar to tossing bread crumbs to the pigeons in Lincoln Park. With similar results, since a small flock of birds came rushing over.

Rajeem and his pack made a scene running through bottles of bubbly even though alcohol didn't have any effect or affect on them. It did have quite an effect on the women who liked that sort of thing. Money has a magnetic pull that draws women like birds to bird feed.

"I'm Shontay!" the lead pigeon introduced to Rajeem once she ascertained he was their leader. She always got the head of whatever crew and left the leftovers for her girls. Just like the lead groupie gets the lead singer while her friends settle for hype men, sidekicks and security.

"Rajeem," he replied and took her hand. He offered an old school kiss on her hand even though he was as far from a gentleman as Mecca is to Las Vegas. Figuratively and literally. His mouth salivated from the smell and taste of a woman.

Rajeem and Shontay engaged in verbal foreplay as he felt her up like one does a melon in the market. She was as plump and firm as any ripe fruit should be. He reached under her tight tube dress and inserted a finger into her vagina. She showed off and gave it a squeeze. Once he got his finger back he took a sip of the juice and knew she would be some good eating. Meanwhile his crew shared mean mugs and snarls with the Lycans across the bar.

Lycans were a superior being to werewolves since they were harder to kill. In even numbers they were too much for a werewolf. They were generally stronger, smarter and more calculating. They could easily kill werewolves with a silver stake or sword through the heart. They evolved with the times and now carried silver bullets in the high tech weapons they produced.

Lycans could be killed as well but it took a separation of the spines to do it. It was that advantage that made the Lycans in attendance snarl arrogantly. They too were on a mission since the Meet Market had the best meat in the city.

"I'm out," Rajeem announced and stood. Shontay stood and wobbled from all the champagne she had consumed. The liquor served as a brine or good marinade would do.

"See you back at the spot," Dog said to his departing back and turned back to their foes. The Lycans had shifted their interest to a couple of big breasted white girls. Alcohol had no effect on them either but turned the white girls red like ripe lobsters. Fitting since the Lycans planned to eat them.

Lycans were usually more reserved than the wild were-wolves. They knew their survival depended on staying off the radar. As long as they didn't make a mess they could pull it off without their leader finding out. Especially since he was all the way on another continent while they scouted this new city.

"Ooh I love to ride!" Shontay cheered when Rajeem escorted her to his bike. She giggled cleverly at her own double entendre and mounted the bike behind him.

"Is that right," he said as he passed her his helmet and helped her put it on. The electric engine whirled to life when he hit the ignition. She wrapped her arms around his torso and held on while he turned the city sights into a blur.

"Mmhm," She moaned and rocked against the vibration of the engine seeping through the seat.

When they reached the Lower East side Rajeem hit a

button on the bike that opened a large door of a loft building. The door opened into an elevator and he rolled straight
on. He hit the same button to close the door behind them.
He hit the top button on the elevator panel and rode up to
the top floor. The elevator door opened right into his living
room.

Shontay almost came instantly when she saw how he
was living. Most of the industrial decor would have to be
admired some other time since he carried her straight over
to the overhead loft where his bed was perched. A remote
caused the blinds to roll up and flood the area with
moonlight.

Rajeem sat her down and put on a show of coming out
of his leather riding suit. Under the jacket was a fitted T-
shirt that displayed his well defined body. He peeled it off
and Shontay fixated her eyes on his abs. She reached out
and ran her manicured nails over them like a washboard.
Then came the dick.

"Oh my!" She marveled at the wood in front of her.

"So much for that myth about light skin dudes huh?"
Rajeem laughed. Shontay just leaned in and gave it a kiss.
She soon had a mouthful and went to work. The woman
ran through a medley of her repertoire of head techniques.
She had more tricks in her bag than Felix the cat but only
made it halfway before Rajeem pulled out of her mouth
and pulled the dress over her head.

"Uh, you gotta eat me first!" she protested playfully. She
was batting around 500 with the demand. Most men
regarding going down on a one night stand like eating food
off the ground. The gritty, grey concrete sidewalks of New
York ground at that.

"I'm going to eat you afterwards," he offered in compromise. That would be a first, but better than nothing. She began to lay back but Rajeem had other plans. He reached down and flipped her over onto her hands and knees.

"I love doggy style!" she proclaimed and put a mean arch in her back.

"More like wolfie style," Rajeem laughed at his own joke as he fondled her box until it soaked his fingers. The juice box was no laughing matter so he leaned back and eased inside.

"I, like, wolfie style!" Shontay managed between firm thrust that tapped on her cervix with each down stroke. Rajeem just nodded since most did even if most didn't get to tell anyone about it afterwards. The pounding that followed sounded like a round of applause as the slap of skin echoed throughout the large loft. Soon her body shivered and shook as an orgasm pulsed through her body.

Lots of men change once they get the pussy, but Rajeem began to change while he was still in it. Shontay noticed the increase in length and girth inside of her. She felt the grip on her hips change sharply as his hands changed to paws with claws. The attempt to pull away only caused the claws to sink into her skin.

"You're hurting me!" she protested. Her pleas fell on deaf ears because Rajeem's ears were growing long. His beard spread until it met the hair on his head, covering his entire face with hair.

The crunch of bone and tendons joined her screams and filled the air as the man transformed to beast. She soon had a full fledged werewolf inside of her. Putting an end to her 'all men are dogs' narrative. This one was a wolf.

Shontay's shouts and screams were sure to wake the neighbors, had there been any. However Rajeem bought the whole building for privacy. Her wails were nothing compared to the sound of the half man/ half wolf reaching a climax of his own.

He leaned back and let out a howl that could be heard for miles. Dogs cowered in dog houses or under beds when they heard it. Shontay tried to scramble away but Rajeem intended to keep his word. He said he would eat her after and eat her he did.

"No!" The terrified woman screamed at the top of her lungs when she saw the beast behind her. An attempt to escape was thwarted by his strong grip.

She wasted another prize scream when his teeth sank into her hindquarters. Predators often start there to prevent their prey from escaping. A satisfying rush of hot blood filled his mouth and fueled his feeding frenzy. Rajeem literally devoured the woman right there on the spot.

This wasn't the only bloodletting in the city. Across town his pack was doing exactly what he told them not to do.

"Is it some other time now?" Beans asked when he saw the Lycans escort their own prey out of the club. He sounded like an exasperated toddler impatiently stalking a snack his mother told him to wait for.

"Bruh," Dog said, shaking his head. He knew there was no talking him down so he stood and followed him as he followed them. He could be the difference that would swing the massacre one way or the other. The driver and passenger split up getting into the front and back seats with one girl apiece.

The six remaining bikes pulled out after the Benz and followed from a distance. Their extraordinary sense of hearing and smell substituted the need to keep eyes on the vehicle. They followed the scent of their prey from blocks away. They all pulled in separate directions and followed their noses.

The Lycans possessed the same powers of sight, smell, hearing, touch and taste but were preoccupied with the feel of tonsils on the tips of their dicks. They guided the blonde heads up and down ignoring the danger lagging close behind. They were under strict orders not to prey on people without permission. The Lycans usually fed on sheep and other farm animals but nothing tastes as tasty as humans. Eating people could be messy in more ways than one. This is why their leader strictly forbids it unless given the order.

Missing persons created missing persons reports, and investigations that could shed light on their existence. They were hard to kill but not impossible. Human hunters could be dangerous if they caught wind of them. The boss wasn't here now so they decided to break the rules. It was only dangerous if they got caught.

"Here," the passenger in the back seat announced when they reached the hood side of Central Park. The driver responded by pulling over and turning the car off.

"Wolves," the driver said and sniffed the night air as they stepped out of the vehicle.

"So? They don't want these problems," the passenger laughed. There was generally a precarious coexistence between Lycans and werewolves. The occasional clash usually resulted in dead werewolves since the Lycans were deadlier. Sometimes it could go the other way when they were outnumbered. Sometimes, like tonight.

"Fuck 'em," the other decided as they headed to one of the wooded parts of the iconic park. It had been the scene of many crimes but none like tonight. They ended up in the exact same place five poor black kids were victimized after someone else victimized a white woman jogger.

The men on their trail peeled off their own riding suits as they walked. Six naked black men walking through Central Park may have been normal, but it was anything but when they morphed from man to beast under the light of the full moon. Four of the six were relatively new to the life and could only turn when the moon was full. That gave them three nights a month to unleash the beast. Dog and Beans were vets like their leader and could turn at will. All six transformed and trotted off in different directions to surround the prey they were hunting.

A homeless man was seeking refuge in a bottle of strong wine when he saw a huge wolf trot past. His eyes went wide at the sight, then checked his half full bottle. He decided he was where he was trying to go and screwed the top back on.

The Lycans reached their destination and laid the woman down. Neither complained when the men took position between their legs without the precaution of protection. Sleeping with strangers from a club was proof of their recklessness so what good was a rubber. The men had just entered the women when werewolves pounced from every direction.

"What the..." one of the women shrieked while the other one screamed. Two of the werewolves snatched one of the Lycans by each arm before he could transform. Dog moved in and quickly bit the back of his neck. The blow severed his spine and prevented him from changing. He clamped down even further until his head rolled away.

The other woman had seen all she needed to see and abandoned her screams. She scrambled to her feet and took off running naked through the park. The remaining woman watched in disbelief as the man who was just inside of her turned into a huge beast. More wolf than man, yet he remained upright on two feet.

The remaining Lycan unleashed a backhand blow that sent one of the werewolves sailing. He landed a hundred feet away before rolling fifty more feet. A blow from his other claw opened another werewolf's torso and exposed his ribs. A roar erupted from his fanged mouth as he took a battle stance.

Dog leapt twenty feet in the air and came down on his back. The Lycan whirled to dislodge him but another wolf clamped down on its leg. He soon had a werewolf on each limb while Beans went for his throat. The last wolf recovered from the blow and joined the pack. He bit down on the back of the Lycan's neck.

The Lycans superior strength wasn't much help against the superior numbers of the wolves. They too were relatively new to this life and got caught slipping. It was instant karma for doing exactly what their leader ordered them not to do. Their car contained enough guns and silver ammo to kill a pack of werewolves. Neither did him any good from the car. He made a break for the car but the six beast attacking him wore him down. Finally Dog and the last wolf met in the middle of his neck and severed his spine. A chorus of howls filled the night air and rippled through the trees like a sudden breeze.

The woman just blinked in disbelief at what she had just witnessed. She was only in search of some dick and ended up with an unbelievable tale to tell her friends. Or not since the wolves suddenly turned in her direction.

"No!" she screamed when most of the pack had turned in her direction. Her next scream died in her throat when Dog bit into it. Blood exploded from between his fangs and soaked his fur. The rest of the pack moved in and began to eat. Except for Beans who took off in another direction. He galloped on all four paws and took giant strides that covered thirty yards apiece.

"What the fuck! What the fuck!" the other woman repeated as she sprinted for the exit. She could see the yellow blur of taxis whipping about and almost made it. She lifted her hand to hail one just feet from the sidewalk. That was as close as she would get.

Beans snatched her into his powerful jaws and dragged her back into the park. He dropped her next to what was left of her friend. Two others joined him and pulled her apart like BBQ pork butt. They devoured the women in between howls that caused regular dogs to holla back with howls of their own

The dead Lycans slowly transformed back into mutilated men. Once the wolves were fed they turned and walked away. They too transformed back into men as they went. They caught up with their clothing and dressed before exiting the park.

"I need a cigarette," Beans chuckled as they headed back to the bikes.

"Or dessert," another joked. Meanwhile, Dog was more subdued. He let out a sigh knowing they now had to deal with Rajeem. Their leader always tried to avoid clashes with the Lycans and only he knew why.

The electric motorcycles whipped quietly down the

FDR, turning heads as they rode. They sped past a police car who decided not to pursue. It was too close to shift change to get stuck filling out reports. That was as good an excuse as any since he knew his beat up patrol car couldn't catch them. They whipped by in a blur of leather while his car smoked like a Philly blunt in a project staircase.

They exited the highway at a high speed and headed over to the building. The same elevator took them up to the roof where they parked the motorcycles. Of course Rajeem smelled them when they neared the neighborhood, so he was waiting when they reached his loft.

"Sup Rajeem," Beans greeted casually as they entered.

"You gonna eat the rest of that?" one of the other were-wolves asked when he saw what remained of Shontay. Rajeem quickly smelled through the distraction.

"No? No! Tell me you didn't?" Rajeem fussed when he caught the unmistakable scent of Lycan blood. He knew it better than they ever could since he was closer to any Lycan than they could ever be.

"We waited for another time, like you said," Beans offered lightly. The look on Rajeem's face quickly erased the smirk twisting the corner of his lip.

"When Arrax comes for revenge I might just let him have you," Rajeem snarled. He knew the leader of the Lycans didn't take dead Lycans lightly. Dog just shook his head and held his tongue.

"Who is Arrax?" another werewolf asked out the corner of his mouth as Rajeem and Dog stepped aside to speak privately.

"His brother," Beans replied. He knew better than most, this could be trouble.

"You think he's going to take the bait?" Dog asked.

They both knew Beans would do the exact opposite of what he was told, just like Rajeem wanted him to do.

"If he doesn't we'll just keep hunting Lycans until he does!" Rajeem snarled. There was bad blood between the brothers although they had once been very close. That of course was many, many moons ago.